PRAISE FOR THE WORK OF
Martin Millar

D0390185

MILK, SULPHATE, AND ALBY STARVATION

"*Milk* is a giddy journey, an amusement park ride, an enchantment like *A Midsummer Night's Dream*." —*The New York Times Book Review*

"The dizzying array of characters and perspectives whips Millar's madcap story into a potent blitz that runs at full throttle through the satisfying conclusion. Fans of Irvine Welsh will love Millar's singularly entertaining tale of suspicious minds." —*Publishers Weekly*

"Creates a patchwork of a novel that is fresh, clever, and compulsively readable . . . Millar's novel so thoroughly embraces its narrator's paranoia that I found myself questioning my own sense of reality. Even so, real or not, I loved this book." —*Bookslut*

"A low-life fairy tale, Milk preserves a strong sense of hard-earned realism . . . one comes to feel thoroughly under the influence of Millar's lively, hurtling prose." —*Bookforum*

"Millar's first novel receives a welcome re-issue . . . evokes amphetamine-induced paranoia without ever approaching a cliché. These days the drugs have changed, but this entertaining fable, which is alternately surreal and grubbily realistic, still delights." —*The Times* (U.K.)

"Pop cultural references are everywhere in this frantic cultish debut which takes an Irvine Welsh-esque turn." —*The Guardian*

"Written in 1987, this welcome re-issue is a masterful work that goes straight to the heart of a spurned generation, alive and not so well, in Thatcher's revolting (in both meanings of the word) Britain . . . A work of rare genius and truly cult, it deserves a place on your book shelf next to Hubert Selby Jr's *Last Exit To Brooklyn*." —*The List*

"Martin Millar created a minor classic with his exciting, surreal and funny debut novel. It is strange, quirky and entertaining to the end."
—*What's On London*

"What's allergic to milk, collects comics, sells speed, likes The Fall and lives in Brixton? Alby Starvation, the first true British anti-hero of the giro generation. A strange and wonderful story, I've yet to meet someone who has not enjoyed it." —*NME*

"A classic tale of Brixton low-life. ****" —*Uncut*

"A crazed comedy of Brixton lowlife, drugs and martial arts." —*The Face*

RUBY AND THE STONE AGE DIET

"I fell a little bit in love with the sweet, gormless, lovelorn Brixton squatter protagonist and his best friend Ruby, who never wore shoes, and who made everything okay by naming it." —*Bookslut*

LUX THE POET

"Millar uses all of the elements of his story . . . to build a batshit atmosphere in which humor and the grim specter of class tension can play."
—*Time Out Chicago*

"An uncommon voice in the wilderness of fantasy novelists."
—*Kirkus Reviews*

"Offer[s] laughs and, finally, some touching insights into life's trajectory."
—*Publishers Weekly*

SUZY, LED ZEPPELIN, AND ME

"Glasgow circa 1972 shimmers like a vision of Atlantis, a lost world."
—Ed Park, *The Los Angeles Times*

"It's like being there, minus the acid." —*Publishers Weekly*,
"Books for Grownups"

"Part romance, nostalgia trip and musical memory . . . a hip and canny gem of a novel wrapped up in cheesecloth and patchouli . . .
[A] heartfelt tale of teen emotional toothache." —*Bookmunch*

"Millar's self-deprecating humor and wild enthusiasm for the music of his youth deepen the pull of this bittersweet read." —*Booklist*

"The British author does a crack job recalling that youth . . .
the mere timelessness of this rite of passage is something well worth documenting." —*The Austin Chronicle*

"A passionate account of what it meant to be young, spotty and in love when Led Zeppelin IV came out, presented in the authentic voice of a dreamy 14-year-old whose other great obsessions are lusting after girls and vanquishing the Monstrous Hordes of Xotha." —*The Guardian*

"His finest." —*Daily Telegraph*

LONELY WEREWOLF GIRL

"It's so compelling you don't want to it end. The grungy, gory, glorious world that World Fantasy Award–winner Millar has created is unforgettable." —Booklist (starred review)

"[A] loving tribute to disaffection and the hopefulness of youth." —*Publishers Weekly*

"Every detail in this book is rich and deep and thoughtful; Millar gives his characters the time and attention they deserve . . . The fact that this is sincerely accomplished through the text is really quite remarkable and a testament to the writing ability of this so very talented, and sharply creative, author." —*Bookslut*

THE GOOD FAIRIES OF NEW YORK

"Read it now, and then make your friends buy their own copies. You'll thank me someday." —Neil Gaiman

"Millar offers fiercely funny (and often inebriated) Scottish fairies, a poignant love story, cultural conflicts, and the plight of the homeless in this fey urban fantasy." —*Publishers Weekly* (starred review)

""Imagine Kurt Vonnegut reading Marvel Comics with The Clash thrashing in the background. For the deceptively simple poetry of the everyday, nobody does it better. Just check out . . . the Highlands-bred, New York Dolls-obsessed fairies for yourself." —*The List* (UK)

also by martin millar:

The Good Fairies of New York

Lonely Werewolf Girl

Suzy, Led Zeppelin, and Me

Milk, Sulphate, and Alby Starvation

Lux the Poet

Ruby and the Stone Age Diet

martin millar

dreams of sex and stage diving

SOFT SKULL PRESS
NEW YORK

Copyright © 2010 by Martin Millar.

All rights reserved under International and Pan-American Copyright Conventions.

This is a work of fiction. Names, characters, places, and incidents are the product of the author's imagination or are used fictitiously. Any resemblance to actual persons, living or dead, is entirely coincidental.

Library of Congress Cataloging-in-Publication Data

Millar, Martin.

Dreams of sex and stage diving / Martin Millar.

    p. cm.

Includes bibliographical references and index.

ISBN 978-1-59376-233-9 (alk. paper)

1. Women rock musicians—Fiction. 2. London (England)—Fiction. I. Title.

PR6063.I34D74 2010

823'.914—dc22

2009043452

Cover design by David Janik

Interior design by Neuwirth & Associates, Inc.

Printed in the United States of America

Soft Skull Press

An imprint of Counterpoint LLC

2117 Fourth Street

Suite D

Berkeley, CA 94710

www.softskull.com

www.counterpointpress.com

Distributed by Publishers Group West

10   9   8   7   6   5   4   3   2   1

dreams
of sex and
stage diving

one

ELFISH, PRETENDING TO be her ex-friend Amnesia, phoned up Mo.

"Mo? This is Amnesia. Remember me?"

Mo remembered. It was more than a year since he had seen Amnesia but she was not a person who was easily forgotten, even by a man who drank as much as Mo.

"What do you want?" he asked, wasting no time on politeness. Mo was never polite. Besides, he hated Elfish and felt no particular desire to speak to her acquaintances.

Elfish was not sure what she wanted.

Her brother Aran, sitting beside her, looked on dully. Aran was so deep in depression that even the unusual event of his sister Elfish phoning up her old lover under the guise of being her ex-friend Amnesia barely interested him.

"Nothing in particular."

Elfish was making some effort to disguise her voice, pitching it a little deeper, but she was not really worried about Mo realising he was being fooled. Elfish's regard for Mo's intelligence was not high. In fact, Elfish's repeated assertion to Mo that he was stupid was one of the main reasons for their present antagonism.

"I'm coming up to London next week. I was hoping I'd meet you again. But Elfish tells me you're not seeing each other anymore."

"Right."

"How come?"

"Because Elfish is a bitch."

"She certainly is," agreed Elfish. "I always wondered what you saw in her."

"I never saw anything in her," claimed Mo. "We just slept together sometimes. I was always seeing other women as well."

"Really?" Elfish forced a little amusement into her voice. "Poor Elfish. I don't expect she realised. She was always pretty stupid about things like that."

"Right," said Mo.

"Well, I'd better be going, Mo. I'll come and see you when I get to London. You remember what I look like?"

Mo grunted.

"I bleached my hair blonder," said Elfish. "You'll like it. Bye."

She put the phone down.

"How was it?" enquired Aran, but Elfish, now on her feet and marching round the room in a tight circle, was too furious to reply.

two

ELFISH WOKE UP in a pool of her own vomit and other people's beer. She groaned. Her head was unbearably sore and it quickly got worse. Trying to raise herself she made it only on to one elbow before vomiting again. It dribbled down her T-shirt, flowing in small rivulets around the already congealed mess from last night. Tears of pain smarted in her eyes and her throat was so dry she could not swallow. When she vomited again she felt as if her stomach was coming out in shreds.

"I'm poisoned. I can't move."

Her groin was damp. Elfish couldn't believe it. She had wet herself. The classroom, one of many in the old school, was devastated. Everywhere were empty and broken bottles, crushed cans and cigarette packets and piles of unidentifiable debris. Some chairs in the corner had been burned and the large classroom window had been smashed. A slight rain trickled through the hole making the broken glass sparkle and the filth on the floor turn to mud.

Good party, thought Elfish, but did not manage to raise a smile. Needing liquid, she began to crawl. As she crawled the fresh sick on her clothes rubbed off on the floor leaving a trail behind her like a snail. Her hand came into contact with a can. Shaking it, she found that it was half full, and drank from it. A cigarette butt flowed from the can into her mouth and she was sick again, followed this time by long shuddering convulsions.

"Elfish," came a voice. "You are completely disgusting."

It was Aba. She stared at Elfish for a while, then leant down to kiss her. Elfish unfortunately could not prevent herself from being sick again. Aba shrieked and spat furiously.

"You ignorant bitch," she screamed.

Elfish laughed, and Aba laughed too. She poured stale beer from the can over Elfish's face and hair and used her sleeve to wipe her mouth clean. She put her hand on the collar of Elfish's T-shirt and pulled. The soaked and rotten material gave way, exposing Elfish's small breasts, over which Aba poured more beer, and rubbed them clean.

"Go away," said Elfish.

Aba grabbed Elfish and kissed her fiercely, lying on top of her so that her thigh pushed into the smaller woman's groin and the studs on her leather jacket dug into Elfish's skin.

Elfish pulled at Aba's clothes but was too weak to remove them, but Aba, who was strong, had no difficulty in removing the rest of Elfish's. Still dressed, Aba poured the last of the beer on to Elfish's pubic hair and began to lick it off.

In the doorway, another party victim, newly awakened, looked on briefly before the pain in his head and limbs forced him to face the daylight and head for home.

Elfish writhed, and wrapped her legs round Aba's head. Aba looked up briefly.

"You stink, Elfish. You stink of beer and whisky and vomit and piss. You are disgusting." She slid her tongue back into Elfish's vagina.

Elfish, still fighting her headache and nausea, managed to unzip

Aba's jeans and slide her small hand as far in as it would go. She could not reach Aba's clitoris but entwined her fingers in her pubic hair. They lay in this manner for some time in the ruined classroom, having sex among the debris with the rain now pouring in through the broken window, turning the mud under Elfish's naked body into slime.

Aba turned Elfish over, wiped her with her sleeve, and licked her anus. Elfish wriggled. Aba slid three fingers up her vagina, gripped her clitoris with her other hand and licked Elfish's anus till Elfish came in a violent spasm that sent fluid spilling out to mix with the sludge on the floor.

Aba stood up, spat, zipped up her jeans, and left. Elfish lay naked and unconscious on the floor, the rain now coming down on her body in a torrent. When she awoke it was midday. She was freezing and stiff, and could not move.

There were many things that Elfish should be doing in the world outside.

I will just lie here and die instead, she thought.

Moments later she began to crawl into her sodden clothes, having remembered that she was Elfish, and the main thing about Elfish was that she did not just lie down and die.

three

IN 1959 AN archaeological dig unearthed the complete text of Menander's comedy, the *Dyskolos,* written about 340 B.C. This is the only complete text of Menander's work that survives.

From Menander, a line can be drawn connecting him with the Roman dramatists, and then to Molière and Shakespeare. So it said in the introduction to Aran's copy anyway. He was interested in this, and wondered who he could relate it to.

His sister Elfish arrived, looking terrible.

"Did you know that a line can be drawn connecting Menander to Shakespeare, through the Roman dramatists and Molière?"

"No," said Elfish. "And I don't care. I've come to use your phone. I'm going to call Mo again and pretend to be Amnesia."

Elfish spat. Her hatred for Mo was intense. Aran produced two beers and they sat and drank.

Amnesia was not around anymore. Consequently there was no chance of Mo meeting her and realising he was being fooled. So Elfish hóped, anyway.

Elfish was as usual both comforted and depressed by her brother's presence. They were good friends, but her brother had entered a clinical depression and seemed to have no intention of leaving it. Elfish, herself melancholic by nature, found this hard to take.

She told him about her experiences the night before, at the party in the old school building.

"I fucked Aba this morning," she added. "Which is good as I know she slept with Mo and I like to fuck Mo's lovers."

Elfish dialled Mo's number, concentrating because the gloom in Aran's room was such that visibility was very limited.

"Hey, Mo. It's Amnesia again. How you doing? I've just spoken to Elfish on the phone. You know she had sex with Aba last night? You see Aba sometimes, don't you? Has Elfish slept with many of your women?"

"So how did Mo take that?" asked Aran, after the call.

"Badly."

Elfish explained to her brother that she was softening up Mo before moving on to the main thrust of her attack and asked him if he would also phone Mo, and drop into the conversation that he had recently seen Amnesia, and she had grown into the most beautiful girl in the world.

This was confusing and troubling for Aran.

"Make her sound like Jayne Mansfield. Blonde hair and huge tits. Mo is so dumb he won't remember she wasn't like that and he'll go for it. He'll go for her as well."

Aran did not think he was capable of doing this.

"Of course you are," said Elfish encouragingly. "And you know how important it is to me. I need the name of Queen Mab."

The thought of actually doing anything at all was almost too much for Aran and he went to his fridge for more beers before relating to his sister yet again how much he missed his girlfriend and how sad he was about it all. Elfish made sympathetic noises for a while till she got bored and left.

Four

QUEEN MAB IS the deliverer of dreams. Elfish and Mo used to play in a band called Queen Mab. They argued and the band split up before playing a gig. Now both of them laid claim to the name.

Elfish was resolute that the name would be hers. It was overwhelmingly important to her. Were her new band to be called Queen Mab, she would be content with the world.

She had no members for her band as yet and although she would undoubtedly find them, time was very limited. Mo had already formed his own new group. They were due to play their first gig in Brixton in ten days' time. Once they started gigging under the name of Queen Mab it would be too late for Elfish. The name would be lost to her forever. Elfish did not intend to let this happen.

Elfish and Mo lived close to each other in a rundown street in Brixton. They were both good guitarists and they were now the bitterest of enemies.

There were various personal reasons behind this enmity, including Elfish's continual assertion that she was a better guitarist than Mo, and their shared habit whilst going out with each other of having sex with other people and then lying unsuccessfully about it, but Mo's main dislike of Elfish came from her repeatedly calling him stupid. Although in Elfish's opinion she had insulted him far more severely than this, it was the label of stupidity which seemed most to upset him.

"No doubt because he knows it's true," she would claim. "Mo is an extremely stupid person."

After ending their personal relationship they had argued violently about the name of Queen Mab.

It might have been thought strange that either of them had ever heard the name at all. It had not been much used since Elizabethan times, and both Mo and Elfish's interest in Elizabethan times was extremely limited. It was Cody, Mo's flatmate, who had brought it to their attention. Cody was a man with both a desire to paint and a degree in English. He had one day asked Elfish if he could use her as a model for a painting of Queen Mab, fairy deliverer of dreams, as she appeared in a long speech in Shakespeare's *Romeo and Juliet*. Elfish, feeling that she was a very suitable subject for anyone to paint, had readily agreed. Additionally, in a rare moment of mutual inspiration, she and Mo had adopted the name for their band; as a name it felt good.

Cody's painting of Elfish as the Fairy Queen, in which she wore her normal attire of leather jacket and filthy rags to match, was coming along very well but had to be abandoned when Elfish and Mo severed their relationship. The resulting hostility meant that Elfish could no longer visit the flat.

Subsequently, however, Elfish stuck by her claim for the name. She had in truth now completely convinced herself that she had thought of it, though in reality it had been Cody. In arguing with Mo she even went so far as to say that the idea must have been hers because she had read the name in Shakespeare's *Romeo and Juliet* whilst visiting her friend Shonen, and Mo had never read a book or a play in his life.

"I know the entire speech off by heart," said Elfish, who had several pints inside her and was thus prone to exaggeration.

"Well, let's hear it then," said Mo.

This scene took place in the pub in front of Mo's friends, including Cody. Cody, from his superior position of actually having read *Romeo and Juliet,* looked at Elfish with particular amusement. Elfish, refusing to climb down, was forced to claim that even though she knew the speech she had no intention of quoting forty-three lines of Shakespeare when she had an important game of pool waiting for her in the next bar. It was an unimpressive lie. Mo and his friends laughed and Elfish was humiliated.

Later, at home, she fingered her moon locket and stared into space. She was angry at being made to look foolish in front of Mo and his friends.

Her moon locket, an old-fashioned silver heart, hung round her neck, lost among rows of beads, and it contained the moonlight. So Elfish pretended, anyway.

O! then, I see, Queen Mab hath been with you.
She is the fairies' midwife, and she comes
In shape no bigger than an agate-stone . . .

Elfish muttered this to herself. These were the first three lines of the speech, as printed in the copy of *Romeo and Juliet* she had stolen that day from the library. On returning home she had learned thirty-three lines straight off without difficulty. She felt somehow that this reinforced her claim, which she would not give up.

five

ELFISH ONE DAY stepped into Aran's motorbike boots while he was sleeping off some depression and has worn them ever since. He used to find this annoying but has now forgiven her.

These boots are twice the width of her legs and she holds them in place by wearing many pairs of socks. Elfish's legs are therefore a distinctive sight, small and thin, with black leggings disappearing into huge boots.

These leggings tightly cover her bottom and above that hangs the leather jacket from hell. This incredible garment was first made for an enormously fat biker, ridden several times round the world, subjected to every stress a garment may possibly suffer, passed through a long string of careless owners, each more wantonly destructive of their clothing than the last, before finally coming to rest on Elfish; a huge, rotting mass of patched, stained, ripped, singed and tortured leather. To prevent its total collapse, various owners have pinned it together with badges, safety pins, kilt pins and sundry other bits of metal, the jacket now being in such a condition that a needle and thread are no longer enough. Elfish has carried on this tradition, adding patches of her own, and also several badges designed mainly to upset the four women she lives with. The right arm, for instance, is largely held on by a badge with the inscription "Nuke Iraq" while the area below the left shoulder carries a mock American military badge with the motto "Kill 'em all, let God sort 'em out."

Under this metal and leather monstrosity she wears as many T-shirts as is necessary to defeat the weather, the topmost T-shirt invariably being of psychedelic brightness, toned down by dirt, and above it her long forelock of hair falls down over her eyes in seven thick strands. These are dyed dark red and black, though rather halfheartedly, and end in clusters of green and blue beads. The rest of her hair is cut very short, and she has three earrings in her left ear and four in her right and one stud and one ring through her nose. For some time she has been considering the current fashion of pierced lips and eyebrows but has so far not made up her mind about doing it.

Elfish is twenty-four, plays the guitar very well, drinks much too much and is of a generally melancholic disposition. Rarely known to smile, she is frequently unpleasant and is occasionally totally hostile. As a friend of the human race, Elfish is a failure. As a stage diver she is a complete success.

At stage diving, which is the art of climbing on stage at a suitably frenetic gig then insanely flinging yourself head first into the audience, Elfish is renowned for her fearlessness. If the gig is good enough, the audience in the moshpit crazed enough, and the stage sufficiently high as to create a real threat to life and limb, Elfish has been known to spend the entire night dragging her small body time and time again past the bouncers up on to the front of the stage, gesticulating meaninglessly to the audience then swan diving blissfully into space, floating free for a brief few seconds before pounding down on the upraised hands of the crowd. If the crowd, generally packed in so tightly that they cannot get out of the way, fail to raise their hands, Elfish crashes on to their heads. If a space in the audience miraculously appears, Elfish crashes on to her own head. It is felt necessary by Elfish, as by all true stage divers, to jump head first, as going down on the audience with your boots would be unsporting, and liable to heavy criticism.

This activity takes up a surprising amount of Elfish's time and, along with her guitar playing, is an effective remedy for her melancholy. Her brother thinks she is simply mad and if they are at the same gig he stands safely at the back and gets ready to call an ambulance.

Elfish likes her brother but her disposition makes it hard for her to bring him any cheer. He always tells her how depressed he is and often she feels that she does not care whether he is depressed or not. Sometimes when he seems overly sad she will make an attempt.

Aran, a writer, had split up with his girlfriend. The fact that he told anybody who would listen that this was too painful an occurrence for him to put into words did not prevent him from trying. He had spent many an unhappy hour telling Elfish all about it, leading them both to such extremes of depression that, when he would finally say that his life was at an end, Elfish could only agree.

"I have no money and many debts," Aran would continue, moving freely on to more general topics. "And even so I am harassed by tax inspectors. I live in a flat which I should not be in, and will be evicted from should the council discover that I am there, which they will when I am unable to meet the rent.

"My best endeavours in the world of literature have led to very little, and I am now being superseded by younger authors with more enthusiasm and better ideas. I suffer from mental troubles of varying kinds, and I have no idea what to do with my life and if I did, I doubt it would make any difference.

"My girlfriend departed largely due to appalling behaviour on my part. I feel old, my face is becoming increasingly wrinkled and my hair is distressingly thin. I make futile attempts to hide this, which makes it look worse. The ragged clothes I started wearing when I was a young punk rocker now make me look like an aged down-and-out. I have become disenchanted with sex, finding it no longer particularly pleasurable, which is just as well, as I am becoming less and less capable of doing it.

"Naturally, being a man of taste, I do not draw attention to these facts in order to generate pity—perish the thought—I merely state them to give you an idea of how I am feeling."

Listening to this grim diatribe, Elfish was by this time thoroughly depressed herself. The thought crossed her mind that if it were not for the fact that he was a regular provider of beer she would never visit her brother at all. Bravely resisting an almost overwhelming urge to flee, Elfish made an effort to divert him from his gloom by asking about his computer game.

This computer game was Aran's new project, or was supposed to be. Roundly proclaiming that books were a total waste of time in the modern world, he had announced that from now on he was going to concentrate on video games. Subsequently he had been trying to program his own game, using his Apple Macintosh computer, in the hope that he could both earn himself a living and educate the masses.

"All games currently on the market are rubbish, fit only for morons," he would say, brandishing his own collection of Sega and Nintendo cartridges and ignoring the fact that he himself spent almost all his spare time slumped in front of his video machine playing them.

"Mere infantile pursuits. I will program a computer game which will be both entertaining and meaningful. My game will elevate video playing from trashy escapism into a genuine and thought-provoking art."

In reality Aran had neither the skill nor the equipment to program a game for either Sega or Nintendo but he did not let this discourage him. He presumed that once he had the thing working on his Apple Macintosh it would soon be snapped up by all the major companies, sold round the world, and possibly made into a film as well.

This was the theory anyway, as he had propounded it at great length to Elfish. Unfortunately in the past few months he had been too depressed about his girlfriend actually to make any progress with it.

"You should carry on," said Elfish. "The idea sounded good. What was it again?"

"The world's main cultural icons from all eras, except the twentieth century, which has very little culture, fall off the edge of the world on a raft and their dreams float up to the moon," said Aran.

"Right," said Elfish. "It's bound to be a winner with young people everywhere. Get to work."

Six

ELFISH HIT MO full in the mouth with her fist. He yelled in pain. "For God's sake, Elfish," he shouted. "What are you doing?"

"That's for sleeping with Angela," said Elfish, and made to hit him again. Mo squirmed as if to leave the bed but Elfish grabbed his balls and held them tightly.

"I'll rip them off," she said, and kissed Mo violently, biting his lip.

"I swear I will kill you one day," said Mo, tearing himself away and rubbing his bruised cheeks.

"I'll kill you first," said Elfish, and they kissed again. Elfish sat up, straddled Mo and crammed herself on to him, forcing his penis inside her so quickly and roughly that they both grimaced in discomfort.

"I've fucked every one of your lovers," said Elfish. "And I gave them all a better time than you did."

"You're a liar, Elfish."

At this Elfish slapped Mo again because she hated it when he called her a liar.

"You are stupid, Mo. Really, genuinely stupid. If I didn't enjoy fucking you so much I wouldn't even bother to talk to you."

"And you're disgusting. When did you last wash?"

"Never," said Elfish. "I stay filthy so I can rub dirt over you."

Elfish and Mo used to fuck so loud and long that the neighbours would bang on the wall in futile complaint. Elfish and Mo would reply with screamed abuse before drinking themselves into insensibility, and waking up ill, but happy.

Elfish's statement that she never washed was not far from the truth. She was genuinely filthy. This was not entirely her fault as the squat in which she lived had neither hot water nor a bath, but the other four women who lived there made efforts to wash at friends' houses. Elfish did this only rarely. Since the crisis about the name Queen Mab had arisen she had not washed at all, deeming dried sweat and caked-on grime to be matters of little importance when there was work to be done.

She sat now, musing on her memories of sex with Mo, playing her guitar on her bed with the TV on, trying to write a song.

seven

THERE IS A legend that everything wasted on the earth is stored and treasured on the moon: unfulfilled dreams, broken vows, unanswered prayers, wasted time. Thus Pope wrote in *The Rape of the Lock:*

> Some thought it mounted to the Lunar Sphere,
> Since all things lost on Earth are treasur'd there.
> There Heroes' Wits are kept in pond'rous Vases,
> And Beaus' in *Snuff-boxes* and *Tweezer-cases.*
> There broken Vows and Death-bed Alms are found,
> And Lovers' Hearts with Ends of Riband bound;
> The Courtier's Promises, and Sick Man's Prayers,
> The Smiles of Harlots, and the Tears of Heirs,
> Cages for Gnats, and Chains to Yoak a Flea;
> Dry'd Butterflies, and Tomes of Casuistry.

Elfish was aware of this legend. It was one of the many random and useless pieces of information her brother insisted on telling her when she visited. No visit to Aran was complete without a long, detailed, cross-referenced and fully annotated telling of some ancient story, lie or legend, whether it was requested or not.

This could be a distressing experience. There can be few things worse to a habitual sufferer of powerful hangovers than to call in on someone simply to beg a beer and a sandwich and suddenly find oneself on the receiving end of a long analysis of the war between Athens and Sparta in 411 B.C. For the unwary it could be a disturbing, even frightening occurrence. Many a shocked young person had stumbled weakly out of Aran's house, white-faced with terror, hunting for the nearest bar in order to obliterate with beer and whisky the memory of Aran's insufferably long description of where exactly the Athenians had gone wrong at the siege of Syracuse, and what he would have done if he had been there to advise the military commanders at the time.

On Shakespeare he was even worse. Elfish still shuddered at the memory of the time she had gone round to borrow some money for a drink and Aran, totally oblivious to her obviously fragile state—post-amphetamine, post-acid and post-alcohol—had declared himself particularly upset by a radio programme he had heard in which Shakespeare's sole authorship of many of his plays had been called into question.

"I refuse to countenance the idea that Shakespeare did not write all of the plays attributed to him," he announced sternly, and proceeded to contradict in meticulous detail every one of the claims made by the programme, leaving Elfish, already in a bad way, more or less a broken woman by the end of it. In a community where the currency of conversation was, entirely sensibly, made up of music, gossip, and a little radical politics, Aran was an intolerable menace.

Nonetheless, Elfish remembered the legend of broken dreams being stored on the moon. It struck a chord in her and she began to think of it almost literally. Each time something went wrong she imagined some wasted effort of hers flying up to land on the moon, and the desire to prevent this from happening again was now very strong inside her. This feeling was heightened by her observation that all around her were people who dreamed of doing all manner of things but never earned their dreams through. Those people who talked endlessly of their plans but did nothing to bring them into reality were particularly scorned by Elfish. She felt that there was nothing she would not do to avoid being classed among them.

She could see the moon from her bedroom through a tear in the piece of dark embroidered cloth that served as a curtain. It disappeared behind a grubby cloud. A movement below caught her eye and she saw that Cary and Lilac were sitting on the grass outside the house next door.

Cary and Lilac were seventeen or so and went around Brixton holding hands and being in love. If they were not going around holding hands they were sitting on their little piece of grass under the moon. This of course was distressing to many folk whose days of innocent love were long since over, and it was particularly upsetting for Elfish. She detested them and regarded them as a menace to her sanity. If there was one thing guaranteed to turn Elfish's general melancholy into a full-scale hatred of the human race, it was a pair of happy young lovers wandering around holding hands or spending their nights sitting in next door's backyard exuding contentment.

Cary and Lilac were making plans. It was their ambition to visit the countryside; in their combined existence of thirty-three years, neither of them had ever stood in a field.

"A field with a cow in it," said Cary. "And some trees."

"And a badger," said Lilac. "And a stream."

They sat in silence, contemplating the pleasant prospect of field with a cow, a badger, some trees and a stream.

Living in the city with a backyard consisting of a few square yards of concrete and an assortment of weeds, where the parks were full of dogs, car fumes and homeless people, this visit to the country was something of a fantasy to them both, though one which they were intent on bringing to reality.

As they had no money, it was not proving to be easy. They were not sure how much it would cost them to reach the countryside but however much it was it would be more than they had.

They were not even sure where the countryside was. Lacking any sort of map of Britain they could only look at their *A–Z* of London, scanning the edges of the outermost squares in search of areas free from habitation. There were in fact no pages of the *A–Z* totally free of roads and dwellings but some of the farthest away ones seemed quite hopeful. Pages ten and eleven for instance, whilst containing a section of the M1 motorway and several other major road junctions, also contained relatively large areas of what appeared to be country-side. Lilac and Cary spent a great deal of time looking at pages ten and eleven, studying with interest bordering on wonder the names dotted over the countryside, names like Levels Wood, Stony Wood and Grimsdyke Open Space.

"Look," said Lilac, pointing his finger. "There's even a farm. Lower Priory Farm."

Cary was excited by this.

"Do you think we could go and look at it?"

Lilac was doubtful, imagining sadly that nowadays farms would be protected by sturdy farmhands clutching shotguns, and possibly even by a busload of policemen waving truncheons. These days this was not so far from the truth. Any movement of people who looked like Cary and Lilac, that is with long, grubby white dreadlocks, ragged hippie clothes and numerous parts of their faces pierced with rings and studs, seemed to induce total panic on the part of the police in country areas. This very day on the news Cary and Lilac had seen travellers who were trying to attend a free festival being hauled away into vans by policemen, and the following interview with the local Chief Constable seemed to them to border on hysteria.

This hysteria was shared by the politicians interviewed later. After watching pictures of young travellers being beaten, kicked and bludgeoned before being dragged away to face charges of assaulting officers in the conduct of their duty, a Member of Parliament assured the interviewer that they were even now formulating strong new laws to deal with this serious threat to society. At the grim prospect of young people going on to uninhabited common land and actually enjoying themselves, the Government was moved to take the firmest action.

Cary and Lilac had been rather bemused as to what all the fuss was about.

"They seemed especially mad that some of the travellers might be claiming benefit," said Cary. "Especially if they were travelling. If you're claiming benefit you're meant to stay home and look for a job."

Lilac made no reply, because he and everybody else knew that there were no jobs anywhere.

They departed quickly from thoughts of the real world and got back to studying their map.

"It would be nice to see a real farm."

There were animals in the city. In nearby Clapham there was a stable with horses next to the railway, and there was a city farm somewhere in Hackney, but this was not the same. It did not satisfy the urge.

"There are still a lot of built-up areas around," Cary pointed out, studying pages ten and eleven again.

"Yes, but remember each page covers a lot of ground. I'm sure if we made it to page ten, we could find a place that was real countryside, and you couldn't see a building anywhere."

"How much would it cost?"

This was a major problem. As far as they could tell from studying the map, the trip would mean a long ride on the tube followed by a bus journey. The fares would be difficult for them to manage. They would also have to buy food for a few days unless they could happen across it locally for free.

Their only regular source of money was Lilac's income support. Cary, being sixteen, received nothing. This was not sufficient to support a couple, even a small couple with modest appetites. On the other hand, they had recently earned a little more from washing car windscreens and standing in Oxford Street giving out leaflets for the Bronte School of English. Unfortunately they had used this money to buy ecstasy and go raving all night, much the same as they had done with the last little sum of money they had had.

"Well, next time we get anything in we should resist the temptation to buy ecstasy and go raving. We should save it."

This they firmly decided to do, and the thought of a few days in the country, even in a place in which the M1 motorway was no more than half a page of the map away, kept them amazingly happy for the whole day. They nuzzled their heads together so that their long blond dreadlocks became entwined. Elfish was fortunately unaware of this plan. Had she learned of it she might well have been driven to violence. Being small, and not brave, Elfish always avoided fighting, but she was quite capable of hurling heavy household objects out the window at any teenage couple she suspected of planning a happy future.

eight

Elfish's main companion in stage diving had been Amnesia, though they were no longer friends. As a stage diver Amnesia had even less fear than Elfish and would unhesitatingly throw herself from any stage into any audience. Whether the crowd was closely packed— the safer option—or thinly spread made no difference to Amnesia. As soon as the guitars were loud enough and the bass thundering enough, Amnesia, already at the front of the audience, would take her head out of the speaker cabinet she was wont to rest it in, claw her way on stage and fling herself gleefully and destructively on to the audience.

Now stage divers were mainly, though not exclusively, male, and while it was still exciting to see some burly eigh- teen-year-old youth hurl himself into space and land on the heads of the people below before disappearing into the mêlée with his legs in the air, it was reasonably commonplace. Elfish and Amnesia being female, and small, stood out, and became well known for their suicidal antics. While Elfish with her hair over her eyes and her metal-patched leather jacket was

distinctive, Amnesia was even more so. She had long stream-
ing hair bleached to a dazzling white and was always clad
in black so that, flying through the air with a beer can still
clutched in her hand and a triumphant curl on her lips, she
seemed rather like a Valkyrie warrior plunging down from
Valhalla. Or, possibly, a Valkyrie warrior being thrown out of
Valhalla for repeated bad behaviour.

If ever Elfish felt herself flagging or became disheartened by
especially mean and violent security men standing in front of the
stage, preventing her from making the ascent, she would be encouraged by Amnesia. Amnesia would be sure to find some way of getting there, even if it meant climbing on the shoulders of some tall
young man and leaping bodily from there to clutch at a speaker
stack. This was indeed a suicidal endeavour. The stack would sway
crazily and show every sign of toppling over as Amnesia clawed
her way to the top. Once there, however, she would be in an excellent position, visible to all, and would spend an extra second or
so waving her beer can at the audience before taking off with an
ecstatic yell. The extra height the speaker stack gave her allowed
her a few extra moments in the air, which felt good, and guaranteed a particularly satisfying crash as the audience, perhaps feeling
that this was a little too much even for them, raised their hands
frantically above their heads to protect themselves from Amnesia's
repeated kamikaze attacks.

Elfish would then follow suit. The pair would continue the process
until either the gig was over or enraged security men bundled them
out of the venue, lecturing them sternly all the while about the grave
risks they were placing their lives in, not to mention the potential
damage they might do to others. By this time, however, Elfish and
Amnesia would be drunk and drugged past caring and would count

the night a success. They would make their way home through night-time London, virulently abusing any men who spoke to them and ignoring the homeless who begged for money.

Tales of their exploits became legendary among the ranks of thrash music devotees, and many a gig was later described in reference to them; people would say perhaps that the band was not all that good, but the two manic stage divers were really and truly excellent.

nine

MO HAD LONG brown hair, one thin strand of which was dyed yellow and held separate by black beads. It fell thick, matted and unclean around his broad shoulders and over his wolf-like face. He was a strong-willed and powerful young man, and in bed he was a wild and cheerful lover.

With Irene Tarisa, herself a guitarist in a local band, he used his tongue without subtlety, pushing it far inside her vagina, up over her clitoris, down over her anus. He licked her pubic hair, grasped it between his teeth till it glistened with his saliva then licked her cunt again with the energy of an animal at an oasis.

Irene Tarisa writhed, because this was pleasurable. She wrapped her legs round Mo's head and sank her fingers into his hair, forcing his tongue even deeper inside her.

Mo dragged himself free, grinned, and in a moment of understanding they reached for the beer at the side of the bed.

Now Irene grinned, and, matching Mo's energy, she plunged on to Mo's cock and sucked it as hard as she could, holding it tightly in a hand that was covered with cheap rings set with skulls and screaming eagles.

Mo's pubic hair ran in a thick diamond far up his stomach and as Irene Tarisa sucked his cock she ran her fingers through this hair, twisting and pulling at it.

After a while Mo, without speaking, sat up, pushed Irene down on her back and thrust himself on top of her. They fucked with energy, Irene digging her nails into Mo's back and buttocks and Mo twisting his head and shoulders to suck and lick her breasts with the same fierce movements he had used between her legs.

While they fucked Irene slid her right hand over her clitoris and rubbed it and in this way she made herself come. She did not make much noise but her left hand tightened on Mo's shoulder so that her nails left deep impressions on his skin. Mo lifted Irene's legs up over his shoulders, fucked briefly in this position then, without withdrawing his penis, turned her over, dragged her hips upwards till she was kneeling in front of him and fucked her even harder than before.

Mo's penis thrust extremely deeply inside Irene Tarisa. Though she would not come a second time, she enjoyed the feel of this, and smiled to herself, her face pressed into the pillow; this pillow, like everything else in Mo's bedroom, was filthy.

Mo, holding Irene's hips so tightly that she was completely unable to move, came in a long and violent shudder. He collapsed sweating beside her, and they lay together briefly before reaching over for their beer. Irene fumbled around in the bedclothes, looking for her cigarette lighter.

Mo was content. Unlike Aran, sex did not make him depressed, and unlike Elfish, he had no devious motives for participating in it.

"Elfish is plotting against you," said Irene.

Mo looked at her suspiciously.

"How do you mean?"

Irene shrugged.

"She must be. She wrote 'Queen Mab' on her front door. You know she won't give up the name for you."

Mo dismissed Elfish's intentions as irrelevant, but his contentment was spoiled by the mention of her name.

ten

STUNG BY SOME particularly biting criticism from Elfish concerning his failure ever actually to do anything, Aran returned to programming his computer game. Unfortunately he was still deeply depressed, so right from the beginning the game had a rather sombre tone, far removed from the optimistic action required by most game players.

In the opening frame the main characters, trapped on a raft, were floating on a vast grey ocean towards the far horizon. They were debating as to whether or not the earth was flat. The point of this of course was that if the earth was indeed flat they would fall off the edge.

Although Aran intended to populate the game with other important cultural characters, he started the game with a cast of four, these four being Botticelli, Cleopatra, Ben Jonson and Mick Ronson. As each of these characters was suffering from depression due to their dreams having departed upwards to the moon, the debate on the shape of the earth was desultory.

"I lost my kingdom to the Romans," said Cleopatra. "It was all Mark Antony's fault. I don't care if we fall off the edge of the world or not."

"Me neither," said Botticelli. "I believed in the teachings of the priest John Savonarola and where did that get me? Into debt. I burned some of my finest paintings merely because he deemed them to be immoral and then what happened? He gets burned as a heretic and I'm left looking like a fool."

Ben Jonson was so gloomy about his theatrical reputation being entirely eclipsed by Shakespeare that he could barely utter a word. He sat on the edge of the raft, gazing mournfully at the waves and bitterly regretting that he had ever composed a complimentary poem as an introduction to Shakespeare's First Folio.

Mick Ronson was only slightly more cheerful. He had had some success when he was alive, notably playing guitar with David Bowie in the Spiders from Mars, but his later career had never fulfilled its early promise.

The inclusion of Mick Ronson, who was only recently deceased, seemed to be at odds with Aran's stated intention of not using twentieth-century characters in his game but Aran had a soft spot for his favourite guitarist and anyway he was generally too depressed to worry about being consistent.

Aran was programing in the hazards for level one. Traditionally in video games these early hazards should be fairly simple to negotiate so that players can get a feel for the game but Aran with his bleak view of the world had no time for easy obstacles. The raft was in theory meant to be making its way back to the shore but Aran programmed in some deadly rocks, hidden under the water. Try as the player might, the raft was unable to avoid these rocks and could not reach the shore. After a long series of frustrations a powerful wind came up, pushing the raft further and further out into the ocean and on towards the end of the world.

Meanwhile the occupants' dreams flew higher and higher above their heads, tantalisingly out of reach.

eleven

ARAN'S KITCHEN WAS rotting away. This rarely troubled him, apart from when he wanted to make tea and he could not find any cups, or a clean spoon. Aran did have many spoons but they were all in the sink with the rest of his dishes and cutlery. The whole mass was usually covered in tea leaves which stuck to the dishes when he emptied the teapot down the sink. Strong people, used to the poor hygiene of Aran and his acquaintances, would still blanch at the sight of this sink.

Unable easily to rescue a teaspoon, Aran poured a little tea from the jar into the palm of his hand then transferred it to the teapot. It struck him that he could eliminate the clean spoon problem by buying tea bags.

Elfish, having remembered that as well as being a good provider of beer, her brother was reasonably intelligent, had come to ask his advice.

"How can I prevent Mo from using Queen Mab as a name for his band, and use it myself?"

"Use it first."

"I can't. I don't have anyone to play with me yet and his new band is ready to go. They're playing their first gig at the pub behind the police station next Saturday. Once they walk on stage as Queen Mab I'm beaten. The name will be theirs."

Elfish screwed up her face in hopeless frustration. Aran, who understood his sister well, did not suggest forgetting all about it and choosing another name.

"Convince him that it is yours by right."

Elfish was not impressed by this suggestion.

"It wouldn't work. Mo is not susceptible to moral argument."

Elfish wrinkled her face again. Aran gave the problem some more thought. Having spent the whole day wrapped in bitter memories of his ex-girlfriend he was pleased to be able to change tack for a while.

His living room was simply furnished, plainly decorated and very dirty, though the dirt was not on a par with Elfish's utterly mangy dwelling. Although it was midafternoon the room was dark. Unable to hang curtains, Aran had blankets pinned up over all the windows.

Aran mused for a while. Captain Beefheart's "Moonlight on Vermont" wailed from his stereo.

"Well, Elfish, you'll have to try and put it in his mind that by giving you some chance of using the name he can make you look bad, and defeat you in some way, which he will like, because he hates you, and also put it in his mind that he can safely do this because whatever it is you have to do to get the name should be something he doesn't think you'll be able to do."

Elfish looked blank, which was understandable. Aran saw that he had not explained himself very well.

"What I mean is, suppose you challenged him to a fight for the name?"

"He'd beat me up."

"Well, yes, but he'd go for it, wouldn't he? And then if you won the fight you'd get the name."

Elfish was particularly unimpressed by this, pointing out that it would do her cause little good to be beaten up by Mo, a man who was three times her size and not averse to violence.

"Learn karate," suggested Aran.

"The gig is in nine days' time, you idiot. I can't learn karate in nine days. This is not a kung fu movie."

"Well, we're getting away from the point here, Elfish. I didn't mean you should actually challenge him to a fight. Just find some way of enticing him into a situation that seems unwinnable for you, then win it."

"What way?"

"I can't think of one."

"Well, that's a great help, Aran."

Elfish was now in a bad mood and was obliged to drink Aran's last beer to calm herself. When Aran made another attempt to give her a brief commentary on Menander's *Dyskolos* her reply was extremely cutting.

twelve

AS FAR AS Elfish could see, everyone around her had either given up hope or had none to begin with. Although all of them were young, Elfish's flatmates, fellow musicians and drinking companions seemed already to have abandoned whatever ambitions they might once have had. For this, Elfish despised them.

With enormous self-belief she made a start on forming her band. The fact that she had as yet no prospect of finding herself in a situation where a band would be of any use to her did not put her off. There were still nine days left until Mo played the gig. If something were to happen which enabled her to claim the name of Queen Mab for a band, she did not intend to be without one. This dream was not going to disappear to the moon.

As there was no time to place adverts or carry out an extensive search for personnel, Elfish knew that the band would have to be composed of people she already knew. This was not an ideal way to go about things, particularly as in her experience Brixton musicians were failures from the day they first picked up their instruments to the day they sold them to raise money for drugs, but she had no choice.

She phoned Casaubon, a drummer she had played with some

35

time ago. She knew that he was always keen to play and asked if he would like the job.

To her great surprise Casaubon said that he would not. He was too depressed even to look at his drum kit any more.

"Why?"

"Marcia left me last week."

"Well, that's the ideal time to play music. It'll make you feel better."

Unfortunately Casaubon was resolute in his depression. Even Elfish, a woman with little sympathy for the world's problems, could hear that he was in deepest misery.

"This is stupid," she said. "I know Marcia. You're always splitting up and then getting back together again. If I fix things up between you, will you play?"

Casaubon clutched at this straw with alacrity. His voice became animated with gratitude as he told Elfish that yes, if she fixed things up between him and Marcia, he would certainly play.

Elfish hung up and rang Marcia.

"Hey, Marcia. I heard you had another minor disagreement with Casaubon. He is a nice guy, however, and he loves you. Why don't you get back together?"

Marcia informed Elfish that they would not get back together because last week Casaubon stole her girocheque, got a female friend to cash it, used the money to get drunk then pushed Marcia down a flight of stairs.

"Is this really so bad?" said Elfish. "Surely you could talk things over?"

"Don't phone me up about him again unless it's to tell me he's dead."

"Right," said Elfish.

She waited a decent interval, strumming her guitar beside the phone, then called Casaubon back.

"Marcia is wavering," she told him. "She thinks she'd like to get back together with you but needs a little more time to think about it. She says she'll come and see us if we play on Saturday and discuss it with you then. How about it?"

Casaubon, his crushed spirit rekindled, agreed happily. As soon as Elfish rang off he went immediately to reconstitute his drum kit out of the pile of junk he had reduced it to by kicking it furiously around the hallway after Marcia departed.

Elfish hurried over to Aran's flat, just round the corner. There was no answer when she rang the buzzer but she was used to this, and kept on ringing it till her brother appeared, looking gloomy.

"Well?" she demanded. "Have you thought of anything?"

"Yes. I have. You must lure Mo into a trap. Use sex as the bait. Mo will be unable to resist."

"What sex? You want me to fuck him?"

Elfish spat on Aran's rug. Aran said no, or at least not right now. He told Elfish of his idea, which involved Elfish pretending to be Amnesia, who had once been her friend.

"A very attractive young woman, Amnesia, I remember. Mo would like her. And she has not been around for a long time."

Elfish drank some beer and listened to Aran's scheme. At the end, she was satisfied. Her brother's plan seemed not unreasonable.

"Would you like to hear about my video game?" said Aran, and Elfish nodded.

"Well, Botticelli the painter, Cleopatra the Egyptian queen, Ben Jonson the dramatist and Mick Ronson the guitarist are adrift on a raft, heading towards the edge of the world. They want to get back to the shore but all these things get in their way and they never make it. Meanwhile, their dreams, hopes and ambitions fly up to the moon."

"Well, I'm glad you're avoiding easy symbolism," said Elfish.

"Do not mock," said Aran. "After all, it was you who told me to get on with it. Look, I'm just doing level two where they are joined on the raft by Pericles, the great Athenian statesman. He gets washed overboard from a passing trireme. He saved Athens in the first war against the Persians but then things went badly for him and he had to flee the country."

"What happens next?"

"They're still trying to get back to land but they can't because a huge sea monster keeps knocking them off course. Meanwhile they drift closer and closer to the edge of the world and if they reach the edge they'll fall off and be killed. Or possibly just set adrift to wander hopelessly forever in endless space. I haven't decided yet."

Elfish tried level two, struggling to avoid the huge sea monster, but it was too difficult. The puny weapons possessed by the voyagers seemed to have no effect on it at all.

"How do you beat it?" she demanded.

"You can't," said Aran. "It inevitably pushes you further towards your doom."

"Well, what use is that? You can't have a video game that you can't win."

Aran did not see why not. To him it seemed entirely appropriate.

thirteen

SO ELFISH, PRETENDING to be Amnesia, took to calling Mo. Mo was usually surly and untalkative but Elfish would move the conversation along by criticising Elfish. Mo went along with this for a while but eventually asked Amnesia why she kept phoning him. After all, they had only met on one brief occasion, some time ago. It was not beyond Mo's egotism to imagine that since then Amnesia had dreamed of him constantly and now wished to bring her dreams to fruition, but if this was the case he supposed that she might as well come out and say it.

Now Elfish was indeed trying to give this impression to Mo but she prevaricated, intending that his desire for Amnesia should make him amenable to her plan. So she did not come right out and say yes, she did want Mo's body, but let the question lie unanswered without refuting it in any way.

As a help, she had already induced Aran to phone Cody, who lived with Mo, and work Amnesia into the conversation. This had taken some persuasion as Aran claimed to be too depressed to do anything at all but he had eventually cooperated to oblige his sister.

During the conversation he mentioned to Cody, without any skill or subtlety, that he had last week run into Elfish's old friend

Amnesia and it struck him as remarkable how much she resembled Jayne Mansfield, and by coincidence she had told him how much she admired musicians, and by further coincidence she was planning to visit Brixton very soon.

Provided that Cody had been sufficiently stoned at the time of the conversation not to realise that Aran was making it all up, which was likely, this tale should now have got back to Mo.

Aran was grumpy after this conversation. This was partly because he had been forced into actually doing something, which he always tried to avoid, and partly because Elfish had absolutely insisted that he stress to Cody the dazzling blondeness of Amnesia's hair and the impressive size of her breasts.

"I can't go around saying things like that," he complained to Elfish. "It will be terrible for my image. If word got out, left-wing publications would stop giving my books good reviews."

"Left-wing publications would send round lynching parties if they actually heard some of the things you say in private about the woman who lives next door," replied Elfish.

She was satisfied with her progress. As a consequence of the phone call from Aran, Elfish now expected that Mo would be prepared to do a little work on Amnesia's behalf because Mo's sexuality, despite having many outlets, was always on the lookout for more. Or, as she put it to Aran, Mo was ruled by his dick.

Elfish continued with her own telephone conversation. "I'll come right out with it, Mo. I want your help in revenging myself on Elfish. You know what she did to me and I plan to pay her back."

Speaking to Mo enraged Elfish and only the knowledge that it was necessary for her cause enabled her to cope with her fury. No degradation was too severe in her quest for the name of Queen Mab.

"Why is it so important to her?" Cody had asked Aran during their conversation, but beyond saying that Queen Mab was the deliverer of dreams, which might mean something to Elfish, and maybe even to Mo, Aran was unable to answer this satisfactorily.

fourteen

CARY AND LILAC decided to save for their visit to the country although the concept of saving was tedious, difficult and completely unknown in their social circles. Realising that it would be a poor holiday with only sufficient money for fares, they determined to save enough to travel, to eat bread and drink cider and exist in comfort for a few days.

"We can find a tree, eat some bread, feed ducks in the stream, drink our cider then fuck on the grass."

This seemed like a perfect arrangement. There was unfortunately the problem of saving money. Not only was this a difficult prospect in itself, but there was the additional problem of Dennis. Dennis was the sole other occupant of their house. He was too objectionable for anyone but Cary and Lilac to share four walls with him, and he had long ago collapsed into alcoholism. When he could afford it Dennis drank Special Brew for breakfast and cider for lunch before finishing off his day by sharing whatever drink was available with the equally far gone alcoholics who sat around in groups on the benches in Brixton Road. Dennis was rather younger than most of them but with his ever-reddening face and lack of control of his spittle he was beginning to fit in well.

It was not possible to save money in a house where Dennis lived. He would not stop to think before taking it to buy drink. And though he was normally to be found with his head on the kitchen floor, dribbling, Cary and Lilac had already found to their cost that in his rare moments of sobriety Dennis was remarkably adept at finding money.

Consequently they decided to hide their savings in their back garden, in a tin, buried in the one small space that was uncovered by concrete. While Dennis was well out of the way, entertaining the shoppers in Brixton Road with his amusing begging, they dug a small hole, placed a tin under the ground and began to hoard their pennies.

fifteen

Shoot an elephant
Fell a tree
Make it into a brooch for me
Of shiny wood and i-vor-y
Shoot an elephant   ·
Fell a tree

This was one of Elfish's songs, though not one that had ever gone down particularly well with the women she lived with. She hummed it as she strolled into the pub and bought a pint of lager.

"How's your brother?" asked Tula, one of Elfish's few friends, as they sat waiting their turn on the pool table.

"Catastrophically depressed."

"Still? His girlfriend left him months ago."

"That's nothing for my brother. I'd give him two years or so before he comes out of this one. Aran stays depressed about things for a long time. He still feels very bad that they changed the name of his favourite chocolate from Marathon to Snickers, and that was years ago. Every time he reads some Ancient Greek history about the battle of Marathon he starts complaining about it again. Says he had no problem at all asking for a Marathon in a sweetshop but he's completely unable to say the word 'Snickers'. It was a very severe blow, chocolate-wise."

Tula nodded in sympathy.

"Well, I guess it will take him a long time to get over his girl-friend."

"He won't ever really get over it," said Elfish. "But eventually the bad feelings will be superseded by some new disaster. My brother is a real mess. But then, so is everyone I know. Apart from Cary and Lilac, who always seem happy. No doubt they will come to a bad end. I hope they come to a bad end. If they don't come to a bad end I will kill them."

A long row of coins lay on the side of the pool table, reserving the next game for whoever had placed them there. In this pub the winner stayed on the table, so that when Elfish's coin came up she had to beat the winner of the last game before she could play with her friend. This she duly did, potting the black while her opponent still had five balls left on the table. He moved to shake her hand but Elfish ignored him.

As Elfish broke in the next game Tula could not help noticing how dirty Elfish's hands were.

"Have you given up washing?"

"Yes. I've no time to go around other people's houses looking for a bath. I'm too busy with everything. After this game I have to find a guitarist who will play everything I tell them to, and that's never easy. They always have stupid ideas of their own."

Elfish was delayed a little, though, because after beating Tula she stayed on the table. She defeated her next four opponents, which gave her intense satisfaction.

sixteen

[STAGE DIVING WITH ELFISH]

Elfish and Amnesia had been close friends for some years. Their friendship ended about a year ago after a gig at the Marquee in Charing Cross Road. They had gone there with high hopes of some serious stage diving because although the stage at the Marquee was not high enough to present any sort of real challenge it was generally easily accessible. While the stage diving might be a little lacking in thrills and audience amazement, it could at least be performed a great many times.

As it was too expensive in the Marquee for them to drink very much they bought a quarter bottle of cheap whisky from a supermarket. They drank it on the underground then headed into a nearby pub before going into the gig. Many people in the audience nodded or spoke to them as they passed because they were a well-known duo. As they stood at the bar, bored with the support act, young boys came to talk to them and offer them drinks. Elfish was in those days clean and was looking good. She drew attention, though not nearly as much as Amnesia, whose long blonde hair, tight black clothes and tattooed shoulders always brought young men flocking round.

Mo was in the audience with some friends. Elfish was at that time having a relationship with Mo but tonight they paid each other little attention, staying instead with their own companions. They could do this without it seeming strange, or hostile.

The band came on more quickly than they expected. As the first notes were sounding Elfish and Amnesia were still elbowing their way through the dense crowd. Amnesia arrived at the front first and was on stage before the singer reached his first chorus. Elfish joined her and together they launched themselves on to the upraised hands of the crowd. The band were popular at the time, and very loud, and before they appeared on stage there had been an excited atmosphere in the hall. Immediately their set began, Elfish and Amnesia's activity ignited the crowd and there was a mass rush for the stage.

The security men were completely overrun and soon there were stage divers everywhere, plunging through the air, arms and legs in all directions, thumping into the crowd, picking themselves up, struggling back to the front and repeating the process.

Elfish and Amnesia were in their element. They were set up for yet another night of glee, and this feeling was shared by many of the people there. The singer's vocals, lost in the badly mixed roar of screaming guitars, were full of disdain for the world and all its problems. He was a man who wished merely to get drunk, stoned, make a noise and have a good time. Elfish was not particularly interested in his lyrics but had she been able to make them out as she plummeted from stage to audience, drink-addled and immune to pain, she would have found herself, for that moment at least, in complete agreement with him.

seventeen

MARION, ONE OF Elfish's flatmates, asked Elfish if she could return the money she had borrowed last week. Elfish brushed aside this request, having no intention of ever paying Marion back. Elfish owed small sums all around Brixton, none of which would ever be repaid.

"I really need it," said Marion, but Elfish merely shrugged and said she was broke, and would try to find the money next week. Faced with this brazen lie, Marion was forced to give up.

Elfish's squat was a large old three-storey house, one of the many large properties to be found in the side streets of Brixton dating from the long-gone time when it had been a fashionable area. The house was crumbling away. The rain leaked through the roof and the wind came in through the gaps round the window frames. Plaster was missing from the walls and the meagre supply of cold water they had made its way slowly from the tank to the tap via a string of rubber hoses held together by metal clips.

None of the five women who lived there felt particularly hard done by, however. Years of living in the area had given them some sort of immunity to bad housing conditions. They rather liked the house and would be sorry when they were evicted, as they inevitably would be.

Elfish wished to phone Mo. She would normally prefer to do this from the privacy of Aran's house but today she was suffering from a hangover and a bout of melancholy and did not feel like leaving the house. Gail was using the phone and Elfish fretted while she waited.

"Are you going to be all day?" she snapped eventually. Gail pretended to ignore Elfish but in reality she was distracted by her rudeness and brought her conversation to an end, as Elfish knew she would. She glowered at Elfish.

"Don't interrupt me when I'm on the phone," she said.

"It's no wonder we get such huge phone bills when you're talking all the time," countered Elfish. Realising that this had given Gail an opening for criticising her for never actually paying her share of the phone bill, Elfish turned quickly and headed upstairs to the extension phone.

A long wire ran from the living room up the stairs to the other telephone. These stairs were a dangerous obstacle course, littered with empty paint tins, cardboard boxes and an old fridge. They creaked ominously at Elfish's footsteps. Elfish manoeuvred her way carefully past the various obstructions but before she could lift the phone some more creaking on the stairs warned her of an enemy approach. As none of the other women in the house liked Elfish she felt quite justified in regarding them as enemies.

"What is it now?" she snapped.

"I need my guitar strings back," said Gail, and her voice was heavy with the implication that Elfish had no right to take them in the first place.

"No," said Elfish. "I need them."

"So do I."

"You never play your guitar."

"Well, that doesn't mean you can just walk into my room and take the strings off it."

Gail marched past and on up to Elfish's room to claim back her guitar strings. Elfish cursed, and wished that the stairs might collapse and bury Gail in a pile of rubble. It struck her that the next time the house was empty she would take Gail's guitar and sell it. This thought cheered her as she waited till Gail had finished removing the strings and walked stiffly back downstairs. It was now time to phone Mo.

eighteen

SHONEN WAS MUCH more pleased to receive a visit from Elfish than Elfish was to be making it. They used to be good friends but these days Elfish generally tried to stay out of Shonen's way because Shonen suffered seriously from bulimia. Elfish found it hard to muster much sympathy for this.

Shonen would eat food and throw it up again at an incredible rate. A visit to her house meant a long series of waits while Shonen made feeble excuses to leave the room and vomit up whatever junk food she had just consumed. Elfish found the whole process most frustrating and could barely resist the temptation to shout at Shonen, "Don't eat it if you don't want it!" although this of course is not the recommended way to speak to anyone with bulimia.

Leaving the room to be sick could happen anything up to ten times in a two-hour visit. While Shonen's bulimia made her feel so guilty about eating that she would be obliged to stick her fingers down her throat and make herself sick after bingeing, she would also vomit spontaneously at times of serious anxiety. This, thought Elfish, added up to an incredible daily rate, unless being in company made Shonen more upset than usual. Possibly she controlled it better on her own.

Elfish explained the purpose of her visit while Shonen sat nervously on the edge of her chair, eating crisps.

"I am obliged to learn the entire Queen Mab speech, as spoken by Mercutio in *Romeo and Juliet,* which amounts to forty-three lines. I need help. I have come to see you because you are an actress and must know how to learn lines."

Shonen was doubtful. Her chosen speciality was physical theatre, in which herself and the five other members of the company would move the story along by pretending to be tables, chairs, cats, dogs and whatever else was necessary. They made up all their own scripts. She did not act in Shakespeare or anything like it, and had not done so since leaving drama school two years ago.

She explained her doubts to Elfish, casually placed her crisp packet on the floor, and excused herself. Elfish waited with pursed lips while Shonen emptied herself of the demon food in the toilet.

While out together at gigs, raves or parties, Elfish had often been obliged to help Shonen out of some incredible situations where old and fragile toilet bowls had seized up completely after relentless visits from the bulimic actress, leaving outraged fellow partiers looking on in horror as a hideous mess of vomit and sludge-like water oozed up over the bowl to cover the floor, making the bathroom totally off-limits for the rest of the night, and possibly forever.

"I know it is not your sort of thing," continued Elfish, on Shonen's return. "And you are generally more at home whilst pretending to be a field of wheat, or the spirit of freedom, but you must have learned speeches from Shakespeare at one time. And it is not nearly as difficult for me as it sounds because I have already learned thirty-three lines of the speech and have a rough idea of how the rest goes. I just need you to do a little final coaching."

Shonen could not understand why this had suddenly become so important to Elfish.

"I have to learn the speech in order to claim the name of Queen Mab for my band."

Shonen looked blank. Elfish explained that she had made an arrangement with Mo, this arrangement being that if Elfish could stand up on stage in front of the audience before Mo's gig and recite the forty-three line speech she could have the name of Queen Mab, provided she had a band to go with it.

"Why did Mo agree to that?"

"Because he is keen to make me look foolish and he thinks that I will look very foolish indeed trying to quote a speech from Shakespeare to his audience, particularly as he is completely certain that I will not be able to learn it in the first place. Already he has spread the word and much of Brixton will be there to see me make an idiot of myself. Unfortunately for them they will all be disappointed because they are unaware that I know most of it already."

Elfish did not further explain that her brother had brokered this agreement through the imaginary agency of Amnesia and that Mo had gone along with it not merely to humiliate Elfish but to gain favour with Amnesia.

"When I am successful Mo will be obliged to cede the name to me."

Shonen looked troubled and opened a packet of biscuits.

"What happens if you fail?"

"Then Mo may demand from me anything he desires. Mo stipulated this condition, saying that otherwise he would just carry on and use the name when he was ready. This is an unpleasant aspect of the agreement but it was necessary to entice Mo into it."

Shonen looked at Elfish in amazement.

"You have entered into a competition with Mo, a man of cave-man-like desires, the prize for which is anything the winner desires? Are you completely mad?"

Not as mad as you, thought Elfish sourly, as Shonen excused herself and hurried out of the room.

nineteen

ALCIBIADES WAS AT the height of his fame around 421 B.C. and he was the most famous man in Athens. He was rich, talented and beautiful. He once entered seven chariot teams for events in the Olympic games. He could probably have had anyone he wanted in Athens but the person he most wanted was the renowned philosopher Socrates, whom he couldn't have.

Plato relates that Alcibiades once invited Socrates round for dinner. There were no other guests, and after they had eaten, Alcibiades dismissed the servants and slaves and started to ply Socrates with drink. Socrates, however, as well as being a famous philosopher, also had a huge capacity for alcohol and did not become drunk. Eventually Alcibiades said to Socrates that it was getting late so why didn't Socrates just stay the night?

Socrates agreed, and Alcibiades, fully intending to have sex with him, covered him where he lay on the couch with a blanket, then got under the blanket himself. Unfortunately for Alcibiades, nothing happened. Despite the fact that Alcibiades was the most desirable man in Athens and had every reason to suppose that Socrates would be unable to resist him, Socrates did not react, and politely declined Alcibiades' advances.

"Isn't that interesting?" said Aran.

Elfish looked blank.

"Why?"

"Because it was two thousand years ago and people are still acting the same, namely asking someone round, plying them with drink and then saying, 'It's too late to go, you might as well stay.' I've done it myself."

"And lost your girlfriend."

"Well, yes, there is that. Possibly Alcibiades suffered the same problem. Do you want to know what happened to him as the Peloponnesian War progressed?"

"Definitely not," said Elfish. Her eyes were already glazing over. She sometimes consented to listen to Aran's stories but she rarely found anything of interest in them.

twenty

THE FOUR WOMEN with whom Elfish shared the old house had tried their best to like Elfish but she made it impossible. They had done their utmost to be understanding but one and a half years of Elfish's continual refusal to pay bills or buy food, and utter inability to wash a dish or clear up her mess after her had worn them out.

In the face of frustrated demands for her share of the telephone bill, a considerable amount, or even a few pence for the soap and lightbulb fund, Elfish would remain calmly unconcerned. Even under intense questioning about the fate of four beers Marion had had in the fridge, Elfish could display a Zen-like calm, refusing to descend to the level of petty household squabbles. Only if, as had happened before, her flatmates unearthed suspicious empty beer cans stuffed in the bottom of the rubbish bin would Elfish become animated, and violently accuse the others of interfering in her business and roundly condemn them for daring to question her word.

They all strongly desired that she would leave the house but as Elfish was among those who originally squatted it they felt unable to use actual force to get rid of her.

This house had once been a place of optimism and activity but it had recently become a dark and sad place. Elfish's dreadful behaviour notwithstanding, the four other occupants—Marion, Chevon, Gail and Perlita—had until only last month been bright and active participants in the projected production of a small independent feminist newspaper. This was to be a journal for young women and the mock-up they had made was a pleasingly chaotic South London mix of extreme politics, music articles and hastily scrawled cartoons.

Now, after devoting almost their entire existences to it, they were facing failure. They could not raise the money to produce the first issue. Worse, they had failed to find a distributor. Even if they could have raised the money, without a distributor the project would never get off the ground. Distribution was a key element, and as any small radical journal such as theirs would never be welcomed with open arms by distributors who were entirely concerned with large volume sales, it had always been a matter of some doubt as to whether they would be able to find one. The only alternative was to distribute it themselves by taking it around bookshops on their bicycles and suchlike but this would get them no further than one or two small outlets in London. This did not seem worthwhile. The whole point had been to break away from such small-scale communication and talk to the rest of the country. Now, after months of preparation and expense they were defeated and had ended up in debt and depression.

On this day, as Elfish arrived in the living room sometime in the afternoon, yawning, Marion, moving swiftly back from national politics to local issues, was moved to confront her about the disappearance of the peanut butter she had bought yesterday.

"Did you eat it?"

"Yes," said Elfish.

"Why?"

"What do you mean, why?" protested Elfish. "We all share food in this house, don't we?"

"But you never buy any."

"I never have any money," said Elfish, logically.

Marion, disheartened by recent events, gave up the argument. Elfish switched on the TV. Television was for some reason an irritating subject in this household. Although they owned one, no one seemed to approve of it. They would occasionally spend time discussing how much they disliked it. Elfish, however, was a self-proclaimed TV fan and during the day would watch game show after game show with blank attention till it was time for her to go out and play pool or re'hearse.

Marion, annoyed, expressed the opinion that Elfish was a waste of time as a human being and a person completely without ambition.

"To hell with you," retorted Elfish. "I dream of calling my band Queen Mab and I am going through extraordinary difficulties to do it."

On the extension upstairs, she called Mo. The very act of deception gave Elfish pleasure. Mo's belief that he was talking to Amnesia when he was in fact talking to Elfish made her feel powerful and was further proof of Mo's stupidity.

The greatest proof of Mo's stupidity of course was that he had slept with various other women while having a relationship with Elfish, and failed to conceal it. The second greatest proof was that he imagined he could steal the name of Queen Mab.

As Amnesia, she was merry on the phone.

"Elfish went for it? She is really going to try and learn forty-three lines of Shakespeare in a week? She can't even remember what day she signs on."

She laughed uproariously. Mo joined in.

"Not that it matters. She won't have a band in a week and that's part of the agreement too."

Mo informed Amnesia that he had already spread word of Elfish's hopeless endeavours around Brixton so there would be plenty of people to see her humiliation.

"What are you going to ask Elfish for when you win?" asked Elfish, but Mo said he had not yet decided.

"When are you coming up?" asked Mo.

"At the weekend. I'll see your gig."

"What are you going to give me for making Elfish look foolish?"

"Anything you desire, Mo," said Elfish, and they laughed again.

twenty-one

PERICLES WAS A natural leader but his efforts to rally the spirits of the occupants of the raft met with little success.

"So your reputation was entirely eclipsed by Shakespeare?" he said to Ben Jonson. "So was everyone else's. It doesn't mean that you didn't leave a great body of work behind you."

Ben Jonson did not find this very comforting.

"And they buried you in Westminster Abbey," continued the Athenian.

"Well, whoopee," said the dramatist, with some bitterness.

Cleopatra leapt to her feet, yelling, "Tidal wave approaching!"

"Damn," screamed Botticelli, who had been trying to construct some sort of steering device to get them back to shore. Botticelli was a poor engineer and wished he had paid a little more attention to Leonardo da Vinci and the other Renaissance scientists.

"Take cover!"

"What do you mean, take cover?" demanded Cleopatra. "We're on a raft."

Botticelli's efforts to guide them safely past the tidal wave proved futile and the vast bulk of water crashed over them, sweeping away what little food supplies they had and propelling them even further from the shore and closer to the edge of the world.

Aran chuckled as he finished programing in the tidal wave. He wondered what new disasters he could send against the hapless mariners. An inescapable whirlpool, perhaps? Or a giant school of killer whales?

A woman with long red hair, tumbling by in the violent ocean, grabbed on to the side of the raft and held on grimly with one hand. Ben Jonson and Cleopatra rushed to her aid while Botticelli and Mick Ronson tried to repair the shattered mast and sail.

The woman was helped on board, bedraggled, gasping for breath but still clasping a mighty sword in one hand. Once on board, she glared suspiciously round her for a few seconds before collapsing in a heap. Cleopatra took off one of her regal cloaks and wrapped it round the stranger for she was wearing only a chainmail bikini, no real protection against the storm. Later, when she awoke and felt stronger, the newcomer introduced herself as Red Sonja, a female barbarian and onetime star of her own comic book.

"But it was only a matter of time before I was cancelled," she related, with a hint of sadness. "Even the film I starred in was not as well reviewed as *Conan the Barbarian*."

So Red Sonja joined them on the raft. Her dreams of success fluttered way above her, far out of reach, and the giant waterfall at the edge of the world crept ever closer.

twenty-two

ELFISH WAS NOT a fan of Elvis Presley but she had a lingering affection for "Blue Moon of Kentucky," possibly because of her moon locket. She could play it after a fashion.

> Blue moon of Kentucky keep on shining
> Shine on the one who's gone away
> Blue moon of Kentucky keep on shining
> Shine on the one who's gone away.

These were all the words she knew, which had not in the past prevented her from playing it onstage in a fast and aggressive-sounding metallic stampede. All of Elfish's music for public consumption was fast, aggressive and metallic. The increasingly popular dance and rave culture had almost entirely passed her by. Elfish had occasionally ended an evening of drinking by hanging around in clubs where dance music played all night, and had even found herself unwillingly trapped beneath an outstretched parachute on which psychedelic lights flickered while ambient music floated all around, but she was not impressed. While the people around her gazed in drug-induced wonder at the colours swirling overhead on the parachute silk, Elfish merely fretted, and wished that the DJ would play a proper record with guitars on it. The thought of making music with machines instead of guitars filled her with loathing and contempt.

Elfish was sitting on her bed, guitar in hand, musing on the prospects for her band. Her ambitions were powerful but she realised they were rather uninformed. Although she knew how to put on a small gig in South London, her knowledge of what might come next was very limited. She was largely ignorant of all the further stages of the music business. She did not know how successful bands became successful. She did not even know how to get a gig in a pub in another part of London. As for reaching the next stage up from this, the independent circuit of small venues, she had only the vaguest idea of what was necessary. She presumed that she would need a demo-tape of some sort but was not sure who to send it to. As for any further progress, to the world of small concert halls, managers, booking agencies, press agencies, one-off deals with small record labels and suchlike, it was all a mystery to Elfish.

This did not trouble her. She knew that she would be able to learn whatever was required when the time came.

As well as the Elvis cover version she had her own song about the moon. The chord structure ran A minor A minor A minor A minor A minor A minor A minor A minor E minor E minor E minor E minor E minor E minor E minor E minor, then back to A minor and so on. The verse ran, "We're landing on the moon, we're landing on the moon," repeated as often as sounded appropriate at the time. She had decided against writing a chorus as it sounded just fine as it was. Back when she had played in her first band, long before she even met Mo, this had always been a crowd-pleaser. She played it now.

Next Elfish retuned her guitar and practised her slide technique, plucking long mournful notes with her fingers, and singing a little blues. Elfish's voice accompanied by the bottleneck guitar made an effective and sad combination. She would never play like this in public, however, and only Aran had ever heard her play the blues.

She could pass away hours in this fashion. It was dark when she placed her guitar carefully against the wall. Summer was approaching and the encroaching heat was already troubling her but the sun was safely gone when she glanced through her window. She frowned, displeased to see Cary and Lilac bending over something in their backyard. Annoyed, she hunted her room for some money to buy a drink, going through the lining of every garment she possessed in case a coin had somehow lodged there unnoticed. This was futile and she knew it because she had been through all these linings only three days ago. After the linings had revealed nothing she got round to lifting up the edges of her rug in case anything had rolled there.

Cary and Lilac were also concerned with money. It is amazing how an enterprise, long thought about, can blossom once finally started. Now that they had got round to saving their pennies the tin was already showing results. Extremely careful not to go near it when Dennis was about, they had now amassed several pounds in their underground store and the prospect of a country holiday was beginning to seem real.

Up above, Elfish found no money. She felt slightly desperate, and wondered if anyone else in the house might have some alcohol. If they had, it would be well hidden from her, and Perlita was hanging around downstairs which would hinder her in making a thorough search.

She picked up her copy of *Romeo and Juliet*, intending to learn the last few lines of the speech, but was interrupted by Perlita knocking on her door.

Perlita smiled at her. She was always smiling. Elfish detested her.

"Someone put this note through the door for you," she said, handing Elfish a scrap of paper with her name on it.

Elfish took the note.

> Full as a Bee with Thyme, and Red,
> As Cherry harvest, now high fed
> For Lust and action; on he'll go,
> To lye with *Mab*, though all say no.
>
> —HERRICK

Elfish was completely bewildered by this. Why had a peculiar poem about Queen Mab suddenly appeared through her door? What did it mean? Where had it come from? Who was Herrick?

She was gripped by a great unease. She did not understand it but surely it was some form of subtle attack. She studied it suspiciously, glaring at the paper as if it might suddenly lash out and attack her. Where could it possibly have come from? Perhaps it hadn't really been pushed through the door. Perlita might have written it herself to upset her. It could be part of their ongoing campaign to get her out of the house. Or it might be from Mo. But why sign himself Herrick? Perhaps Herrick was the name of Mo's new drummer and Mo had recruited him solely to write unsettling poems and send them to Elfish. She pondered it for a long time, pacing up and down in her small dark room.

Eventually Elfish noticed that her copy of *Romeo and Juliet* was still in her hand. Remembering that she had been about to finish learning the speech she tossed the mysterious note on the floor. She tried to put her disquiet out of her mind and run through the large portion of the speech she already knew before studying the few remaining lines.

> O! then, I see, Queen Mab hath been with you.
> She is the fairies' midwife, and she comes

In shape no bigger than an agate-stone
On the fore-finger of an . . .

Elfish came to a halt. A small tremor of panic ran over her as she realised that she could not remember any more. The shock of receiving the poem seemed to have driven it right out of her memory.

twenty-three

SHONEN FORGOT TO water her plants for several weeks, being too upset by the general state of her life to care for them. They all died, despite a strenuous last-ditch campaign to turn things round with food, water, love and attention.

Another disaster, she thought, and it ran easily through her mind that it was no wonder that a person with bulimia should be incapable of looking after plants. Dying plants was only one manifestation of the complete inability she felt to do anything at all.

Shonen's compulsive eating and vomiting was worsening under pressure. The clerk at the social security had just warned her about coming in late to sign on. It would be two days before she got her next girocheque and she had no money whatsoever. In total desperation she had even looked around the shelves of job opportunities at the jobcentre but there were no jobs there. If there had been, Shonen would not have felt well enough to take one, or even to apply.

Her theatre group had just failed to win a grant from the Arts Council. Their projected autumn tour was now cancelled and there was talk of disbanding. At this moment Shonen should be sorting through her directory of organisations which gave grants and making ready a list to present to her fellow performers, but it seemed like too much trouble. The overwhelming probability was that no one would give them any money. They would be unable to carry on.

Shonen had always wanted to participate in a small theatre group which was run by the performers themselves. She was surprised that the ambition of a lifetime could evaporate so quickly.

Having an irresistible urge to eat she filled herself up with apples. She was not particularly fond of apples but as they contained relatively few calories it made her feel not quite so bad inside to be eating them.

Still, it made her feel bad enough to vomit them up right afterwards, and as she stood by the toilet, flushing it rather sadly, it occurred to her that her life was really not going very well. For someone of only twenty-three she seemed already to have amassed many problems.

The phone rang. It was Elfish bearing news.

"Shonen, I was right. The woman in the house next door does work as a professional fund-raiser for the theatre. As I said, she owes me a favour for saving her cat from a tree. And, by a lucky chance, she is a particular fan of physical theatre. She says she'll help you get your group back on the rails."

Shonen felt transformed by this small ray of sunshine. In common with the rest of the world she was eager to grasp at any straw which might rehabilitate her dreams. Consequently she failed to reflect that the chances of there being a professional theatrical fund-raiser living next door to Elfish were slim, and the likelihood of Elfish having climbed a tree to save her cat was zero.

The prospect of a revival in her theatrical fortunes revived her spirits entirely. She went first to her pile of sponsorship forms which she sorted into some sort of order, and next to the trunk where she kept all her old texts from drama school. Down near the bottom she found a copy of *Romeo and Juliet.* Helping Elfish with the speech did not now seem so difficult.

Back in Aran's flat, Aran was frowning at his sister.

"Does it make you feel at all bad, lying to people like that?" he asked, as Elfish put his phone down.

"Not at all," said Elfish. "I had to tell Shonen something positive or she'd never get up the energy to help me."

"What about when she discovers you're lying?"

Elfish shrugged.

"Well, by then I'll have what I want, so who cares? And I really need Shonen's help now because I've forgotten the speech."

"What?"

"I've forgotten it."

Aran was sitting down, but had he been standing he would have reeled in shock. This was obviously a disaster. The whole carefully worked-out plan depended utterly on Elfish knowing forty-three lines of Shakespeare in one week's time. Anything less would lead to total defeat.

"Well, why did you forget it?"

Elfish fumbled in her pocket and produced a scrap of paper.

"Because of this," she said angrily, and thrust the paper at her brother.

"Someone pushed it through the letterbox and I was so upset worrying about where it came from and what it meant that not only could I not learn the end of the speech, I forgot all the rest as well. And I can't remember it today either."

Aran studied the note.

"Who is this Herrick and why is he shoving poems through my front door?" demanded Elfish. "And what's all this about lying with Mab? Is that meant to refer to me? The man must be some sort of freak."

Elfish began to work herself up into a tantrum.

"Calm down," said Aran. "Herrick does not want to lie with you. He's been dead for three hundred years. He was a poet. This is an extract from one of his poems."

"Oh."

Elfish calmed down a little.

"Then what does it mean?"

Aran asked if it had been written by Mo but Elfish could not remember ever having seen Mo's handwriting. Also, she said, Mo would never have heard of any seventeenth-century poet either.

"But Cody would," Aran pointed out. "He is fairly knowledgeable about literature. Not as knowledgeable as me, of course. I imagine that he and Mo deliberately found an obscure Queen Mab poem and sent it to you. Possibly they're suggesting that they know more about Queen Mab than you do. Possibly it was just meant to upset you."

"What a stupid idea," Elfish said with contempt.

"Well, it worked, didn't it?"

"Absolutely not," said Elfish, and stormed through to the kitchen to find a beer.

"Still," said Aran later, "I don't understand why it has upset you so much that you've forgotten the entire speech."

Elfish did not understand this either, but had Mo been there to join in the conversation he could have told her. He recalled very well the time that Elfish had been trying to learn a long set of lyrics the night before a gig and had failed utterly, despite the fact that normally the learning of lyrics did not cause her any problems. Elfish, for all her determination, could not learn lines under pressure. She had demonstrated this several times in the past. In her determination to outsmart Mo, she had neglected to remember this. Mo had not forgotten, which was why he had gone along with the scheme, and was even now spreading the word to his friends about the debacle that was to come. He knew that the pressure would get to Elfish, and he knew that sending her the poem would add to it.

"No doubt it was a temporary failure only," said Aran hopefully. "You'll remember it all soon."

Elfish teetered on the brink of depression, but checked herself in time.

"No doubt," she said. "Meantime I must pay Mo back for this attack. I thought Shakespeare was the only person to write about Queen Mab and now I find this Herrick did as well. Are there any more obscure Queen Mab poems in the language?"

"I'm not sure," admitted Aran. "There might be."

"Then please find me one so I can put it through Mo's letterbox. I refuse to let him think that he knows more than me about Queen Mab."

Aran was about to object that finding an obscure Queen Mab poem for Elfish sounded very much like the activity which he was determined to avoid, being still concerned with his overwhelming depression, but he stopped himself. He did not wish to disappoint his sister. Besides, obscure literary research was always fairly appealing to him, provided he had someone to show off the results to.

Elfish went off to practise. Aran thought about starting the search for a poem but decided it would be unwise to rush into anything. Too much sudden activity might well be injurious to his health. Instead, he thought about his cigarette cards. The brand of cigarettes he smoked were now running a promotion in which each packet contained a card. These were copies of adverts for the cigarettes and were of such artistry that they had won coveted awards from the advertising industry's panel of top artistic directors.

There were twenty of the cards and anyone who collected all twenty could send them off and claim a prize of five pounds. Aran had three cards and had intended collecting the set and claiming his free five pounds but general listlessness and depression had prevented him from making much progress.

He made some calculations. These revealed that even at his normal rate of smoking it would not take him long to collect the entire set. Possibly he could smoke a little more to hurry things along. This seemed like quite a pleasing prospect.

The phone rang. It was Elfish.

"Stop sitting around uselessly," she said. "Get out there and find me a poem."

twenty-four

The band thrashed their way through their set. Their songs were simply structured but they played the chords extremely fast, so fast that all that was discernible was a continuous deep roar of brutal guitar noise punctuated occasionally by fleeting, shrieking high-pitched solos.

Elfish and Amnesia continued to dive from the stage. After one particularly violent landing Elfish found herself wrapped around various pairs of feet and a full beer can and she shared this with Amnesia before making their next assault.

The band played louder and faster, the audience danced and shouted and the support band appeared through a door in the back of the stage to sit behind the drummer, tapping their feet and smoking joints. With the stage crowded and Elfish, Amnesia and the other divers in full cry, it was a very active event, and fun for all. Elfish's melancholy departed entirely when she was midway between the stage and the upturned hands of the crowd. As she thudded on to their heads and disappeared from view into the heaving mass of sweating bodies, she could even be seen to smile.

"*I regard this stage diving as very dangerous,*"*Aran told her, often, but as Aran was dull enough to make a joke that possibly the stage diving could be regarded as a Brechtian interruption between the performers and the audience, and then repeat this joke whenever he remembered it, she did not listen to his views too closely.*

Amnesia was jumping further than Elfish. She made one spectacular leap after another. Elfish could never quite match her. After one prodigious jump Amnesia found herself wrapped around Mo who was enjoying himself in the moshpit, violently crashing into everyone around him. Elfish saw this from the stage and frowned a little at the sight of Mo helping Amnesia to her feet in what seemed to be an unnecessarily intimate manner, that is by her breasts, but she ignored it, and tried to jump as far. She failed in this but it was a good jump nonetheless, and she crashed down again, pummelling the heads of the crowd and moving a few yards along their hands before turning upside down and sliding down through them to the floor. She fought her way to her feet and began to use her elbows in pursuit of Amnesia who was already back at the front of the stage, negotiating the bouncers.

twenty-five

"AFTER COUNTLESS HOURS of difficult and laborious research I have managed to unearth another Queen Mab poem," said Aran, proudly handing a sheet of paper to Elfish. "It was published in 1648," he added, superfluously.

Elfish examined the poem.

> If ye will with *Mab* find grace,
> Set each Platter in his place:
> Rake the Fier up, and get
> Water in, ere Sun be set.
> Wash your Pailes, and dense your Dairies;
> Sluts are loathsome to the Fairies:
> Sweep your house: Who doth not so,
> Mab will pinch her by the toe.
>
> —HERRICK

Elfish was slightly suspicious of this, feeling that possibly all this talk of sluts and uncleanliness might be aimed at her, but Aran assured her it was not.

"It just so happened that the only Mab poem I could find was about being clean and tidy. What's wrong? You don't seem very pleased."

Elfish admitted that she was a little disappointed because the poem was by the same person who had written the verse Mo sent to her.

"I was hoping for something even more obscure than Herrick so that Mo would know I could not be intimidated by Cody's learning."

"I'm sorry, Elfish, it was the best I could do. I spent hours searching and of course I'm an expert at this sort of thing. I don't think there are any more poems about Mab."

What Aran had actually done was walk reluctantly to the library and flick through a volume of Herrick's collected works. It had taken him no more than fifteen minutes but he knew that Elfish was not going to realise this. He figured that this counted as quite a lot of work anyway, particularly as he should have been at home watching daytime television.

Elfish shrugged.

"Well, it will do anyway. No doubt when Mo sees this he will be filled with terror and remorse, and realise that I am well on the way to another success. Not that there was ever any doubt about me succeeding anyway."

"So have you learned the rest of the speech?"

"Well, no," admitted Elfish.

"Have you remembered the bit you forgot?"

"Only up to line two. But I'm sure I'll do better tonight. Before that though I have to go and see May who lives on the Tulse Hill estate. I've heard she's a good guitarist so I'm going to recruit her. What's her address?"

Aran frowned. May was not a good memory for him. She had been one of his attempts to seek physical comfort after his breakup with his girlfriend.

"What's the matter? Can't you remember the address?"

"Yes I can." Aran frowned.

"But it is not a very nice memory apparently. Why not?"

Aran drummed his fingers on the armchair he occupied, raising a small cloud of dust.

"She's in a bad way. We went to bed after a party and when I was undressing her she burst into tears."

"So the rumours about you are true," sniggered Elfish.

"I was entirely free from blame. The problem was she couldn't bear to let anyone undress her because it reminded her too much of being strip-searched in jail in Northern Ireland. She was on remand in prison for joyriding and in that month she was strip-searched five times before they found her not guilty and let her go.

"The last time was a big search involving women officers in riot gear and the prisoners tried to protest. May was thrown on the floor and got her head banged and her clothes ripped off. Male officers were walking up and down the corridor outside looking in and making comments. May ended up with bruises on her back, and a swollen face. She says she came to England to get over it but from the way she started crying at the memory I'd say she has some way to go."

Another sicko, thought Elfish, with some disgust.

"Well, that's fine," she said. "Playing guitar with me is just the thing to bring her out of it. Or not, as the case may be. Just so long as she can play, I don't care."

Elfish left Aran's intending to have another attempt at memorising Shakespeare before visiting May but was sidetracked after meeting Tula for a lunchtime game of pool and finding that she had just been paid for four days' work delivering telephone directories.

"I must go," said Elfish. "I have important things to do this afternoon."

"Have another pint," said Tula. "You're so busy these days we never see you. Play some pool."

Elfish was a fine pool player with a gentle touch, capable of imparting backspin or sidespin to the cue ball to bring it back into position, a feat beyond the abilities of most part-time bar room players. With her leather jacket and motorbike boots she looked good at the table, which she knew.

Playing pool and drinking was fine but afterwards she fell asleep at home and did not wake up until three in the morning. She cursed herself. She had meant to visit May. Now another day had slipped by and she had not made the progress she should. How was it that a person with her iron determination could be so easily distracted? She was engulfed by the overwhelmingly gloomy thought that she might turn out like everyone else and let her dreams evaporate into nothing. Even now they might be flying up to land on the moon.

She walked up and down her room reading Shakespeare and found that she was unable to take in a single line. She cursed *Romeo and Juliet* for being a remarkably stupid play written in remarkably stupid language. Depression set in. In the middle of the night her prospects of success seemed remote. There was too much for her to do. Unable to get back to sleep Elfish lay on her bed and felt bleak.

twenty-six

AS FAR AS John Mackie could remember, he had lit a candle in church for his sister every day for the past fifty years. These candles lay next to an altar in his local Catholic church. They were small and white, encased in thin metal. Beside them there was a box to put money in. Each candle cost fifteen pence.

He was now sixty. He had been ten and his sister eight when they were evacuated from wartime Britain as passengers on a ship to Canada.

The ship was torpedoed and sank quickly. Many people died, including his sister. John Mackie's last memory of her was the sight of her long dark hair drifting away from him in the water while he clawed his way frantically towards her. A wave had separated them and he never saw her again. He had been dragged aboard a lifeboat, semi-conscious, but his sister was never found. This had spoiled his life.

He now ran a secondhand music store in Brixton and was doing badly. For the past ten years he had been fighting a losing battle with the large and modern secondhand store up the road. Their window was packed full of guitars and amplifiers, synthesisers, samplers, sequencers and modern recording equipment, while his was a fairly sorry mix of guitars, banjos, cheap effects boxes and secondhand cassettes that no one wanted.

Anyone with money requiring good equipment would go uptown to buy it new in Denmark Street and anyone short of cash who wanted to choose from a wide variety of goods would go to the other secondhand store. This left John Mackie with few customers.

Standing quietly behind the counter, he started slightly as Elfish entered. He was used to the strangely clad youth of Brixton entering his shop, these being some of the people with very little money who were likely to be his customers, but the sight of Elfish's small figure swamped by her vast, metal-decorated leather jacket still took him by surprise, particularly as her face was almost entirely hidden behind her beaded hair. When she stood at the counter her beads rested on the stud and ring which pierced her nose. She brushed her hair back, revealing her face, which was very dirty. John Mackie felt uncomfortable.

Elfish asked if she could see a guitar that was hanging in the window. There was very little room in the shop, and bringing out the guitar, plugging it into an amplifier and getting it round Elfish's neck was something of a struggle.

Elfish strummed it to see if it was in tune, and then picked out the rhythm of "Green River Blues," a very old tune. John Mackie recognised this tune and was surprised to find someone like Elfish capable of finger-picking it. He almost warmed to her till she abandoned it abruptly, turned up the volume to produce dreadful distortion through the small amp, and played a few savage bar chords.

John Mackie winced. He would never entirely get used to this sort of thing. Elfish liked the guitar but, as was no surprise at all to the shopkeeper, she could not afford it.

"Let me take it now. I'll pay it up."

"No," said John Mackie.

"It is of immense importance to me to have this guitar now," said Elfish, seriously.

John Mackie shook his head. His demeanour was not friendly. He desired that Elfish should leave the shop as quickly as possible because he now realised that his discomfort at her presence was due to the fact that when she brushed her hair back her face bore an uncomfortable resemblance to that of his long-dead sister.

Elfish could not persuade him to part with the guitar. He would not let it out of the shop until it was fully paid for and Elfish could not afford it. Back in her house Elfish was angry. She needed the guitar for May but could see no way of obtaining it.

With no prospect of solving this problem, Elfish hunted around for someone on whom she could take out her bad feelings. She went downstairs intending to pick an argument with Marion, Chevon, Gail or Perlita, either separately or all at once, but no one was around. Chevon's cat wandered in. Elfish was quite prepared to take her bad feelings out on the cat, figuring that any cat that was prepared to stay with Chevon deserved a fair amount of abuse. She prepared to swing her boot at it but the cat was wise by now to Elfish and departed swiftly.

Elfish peered hopefully out the back, wishing that Lilac and Cary were around so she could upset them by swearing at them, but they were nowhere to be seen.

She was now completely frustrated. She felt that she simply had to be unpleasant to someone.

Bad thoughts of Mo invaded her mind, and with them came an excellent idea. She dived to the phone and dialled his number.

"Hi, Mo, this is Amnesia. Elfish has just been on the phone to me. She obviously doesn't realise how much I hate her. Is it true what she told me, that she's all ready to go with her band, and she's going to collect the name of Queen Mab for herself? Pretty silly of you to make that agreement and let her get away with it, Mo."

Mo said that Elfish would do no such thing but Amnesia made light of his protests.

"I'm starting to think that Elfish may be too much for you, Mo. Is it true she's slept with all your lovers and they all say it was better than you?"

"Certainly not," said Mo, with feeling.

"She says you used to drink so much you could never really do it properly. I do remember you drank a lot, Mo. You'd better watch it, you have a few failures and word gets around. And a reputation for impotence is a hard one to get rid of. Oh well, I expect Elfish was lying. Bye."

After this Elfish felt somewhat better. These were deadly insults to Mo and he would now be seething.

This small triumph made Elfish feel like playing a game of pool. It struck her suddenly that she had no one to play with. She seemed to have misplaced all of her friends apart from Tula and she would be working just now.

Though Elfish did not like to face it too consciously, she had in reality very few friends. She had never been a member of a wide social circle. She never went off drinking or dancing with a crowd of people as did the other women she lived with. What acquaintances she had she tended to drive away either through gradually wearing out their charity with her persistent melancholy or banishing their goodwill in a flash of bad temper.

This relative solitude was something she shared with Aran although it was not something they ever discussed. It would indeed be a difficult thing to discuss, even with her brother, but since her terminal disagreement with Amnesia, Elfish had been close to no one except Aran. As Aran was generally too wrapped up in his own depressions and anxieties to be much of a friend, Elfish's life tended to be lacking in light relief.

twenty-seven

MO LOUNGED IN a pub in Brixton, pint in hand, satisfied after a successful rehearsal. He and the rest of his band were discussing management. After several semi-successful forays into music, Mo now felt he had enough experience to find some management, someone who might be willing to pay a company to do some publicity for them. It would be nothing extravagant but might well be enough to get them on their way.

"I'll do some phoning round next week," said Mo.

"Why not now?"

"Because of the name."

The drummer was puzzled.

"I thought you'd settled on Queen Mab."

"I have," said Mo. "But it will take another week to be finalised. There is the matter of Elfish."

None of the rest of the band understood this. They could not see why he did not just adopt the name immediately. If Mo liked it there was no hindrance to him using it.

"Who cares if it upsets Elfish? Elfish is a total fuck-up."

Mo took off his leather jacket and slung it over his chair. It fell on the ground and he let it lie. Over his torso a ragged blue T-shirt strained against the width of his shoulders.

"I want to make her feel even worse than she does already," said Mo, and the others took this as a reasonable explanation. Mo's dislike for Elfish was well known, and if it seemed to have grown in the past few days there was nothing remarkable in that. Everyone at the table had at one time or another felt their hatred and disgust for former lovers grow without warning.

"Is she really going to stand up before our gig and recite a speech?"

"Yes, she is."

Everyone laughed.

"What if she succeeds?"

Mo assured them that she would not. He had experience of Elfish and was confident of her inability to learn lines under pressure.

A thin, black-clad woman with long blonde hair and tattooed shoulders walked into the pub, causing the heads of all the band to swivel.

"I know her," said Cody. "That's Amnesia. I thought she'd left London."

twenty-eight

ELFISH WAVERED BETWEEN going out and getting on with things or spending the whole day in bed. It was vital to her endeavours that she kept busy. Unfortunately she did not feel like keeping busy.

She had a new bottle of whisky, cheap from the supermarket. To bring the television up to her room, stay under the blankets, drink whisky and pretend to learn the speech was a powerful temptation.

Eventually, late in the day, she dragged herself up. She was wearing several T-shirts and many pairs of socks. Both the T-shirts and the socks were ragged, dirty and caked in ages-old sweat. She pulled on her leggings, stuffed her feet in her boots and manoeuvred her arms through the ripped lining of her leather jacket.

Outside the sun shone and Elfish squinted in disapproval. She hated it when the sun shone brightly. It hurt her eyes, even when they were covered by her hair.

"Hello, Elfish," came one cheerful voice, followed by another.

Cary and Lilac were standing outside, holding hands.

Elfish came to a halt, glowering. She could not be sure but she had the distinct impression that the young lovers were gently squeezing each other's hands in a secret message of devotion.

This was too much for Elfish. She glared evilly at them, stormed back into her house, grabbed the television from the living room and marched upstairs.

She brought out her bottle of whisky and, without removing her leggings, boots or jacket, switched off the light and got into bed. She passed the afternoon watching game shows and soap operas, drinking whisky and smoking joints, all the time sinking into a grimmer and grimmer mood till eventually she drank and smoked enough to lose herself in unconsciousness and bad dreams.

Outside, unaware of the dire effects their embraces had wrought, Cary and Lilac were about to embark on a mission to earn money. Even now they were gathering up buckets of water and clean cloths in preparation for standing at crossroads and harassing motorists into having their windscreens cleaned whether they liked it or not.

twenty-nine

"THIS IS HOPELESS," complained Cleopatra, and it was. One might have thought that with the occupants of the raft being who they were, they would have done better against the adversaries who continually battered them. Pericles and Red Sonja were both notable warriors. Cleopatra had received military training and had commanded a fleet at the Battle of Actium. Even Ben Jonson had been a handy man in a tavern brawl. However, their efforts at fighting back were completely futile.

The problem was that their enemies were just too strong for them. Every effort to steer the raft back towards the shore was thwarted. Every time Botticelli rigged up a rudder a sea monster would emerge to destroy it or a winged gryphon would plummet from the sky to rip it to shreds. Red Sonja slashed this way and that with her broadsword but for each gryphon she killed two more would appear.

Mick Ronson had by this time more or less given up and sat in the middle of the raft playing his guitar, which did not really please anyone else.

"I can see it!" screamed Botticelli.

"What? What?"

"The edge of the world!"

Mick Ronson laid down his guitar and gazed at the horizon with amazement. As an inhabitant of the twentieth century he had been convinced that the world was round and had no edge but sure enough, some way off, there was a mighty foaming waterfall which could only be the place where the ocean disappeared into the endless void.

"Get busy on that steering device," commanded Cleopatra, and leapt to lend her weight to Red Sonja who was busy trying to hold off the squadron of gryphons which harassed Botticelli as he laboured. But as two more appeared for each one killed the sky was soon full of the terrible creatures. Botticelli was forced to retreat and the rudder was once more smashed. The raft swept inexorably on towards the edge of the world.

"This is ridiculous," said Elfish, grimly working the controls in front of Aran's terminal. "How do you beat these gryphons?"

"You can't," said Aran. "They're too powerful."

"Well, that's no fucking use, is it?" complained Elfish, standing up in disgust.

"I think it makes for an excellent game," said her brother.

"I think it's stupid. And what am I doing playing your dumb video game? I'm meant to be learning a speech. Today I got to line five and then it all went out of my mind again. I've only got six days left."

Elfish departed, guilty and angry at herself for wasting time. Aran was sorry at her distress but was quite pleased to be left alone to get on with his computer game.

He was just programming in a new character, Bomber Harris, who appeared from the sky after being kidnapped by a pterodactyl, when his labours were interrupted once more.

It was Elfish again.

"Look at this!" she wailed, practically knocking Aran down in her haste to get from his front door through to his kitchen. Aran took the piece of paper she had thrust at him and followed her to the fridge where he found her desperately emptying beer into her mouth. Elfish finished one can and moved on to another while Aran read the note.

> I am the Fairy Mab: to me 'tis given
> The wonders of the human world to keep:
> The secrets of the immeasurable past,
> In the unfailing consciences of men,
> These stern, unflattering chroniclers, I find.
> —SHELLEY

"Well?" demanded Elfish.

"Lousy poem," said Aran. "Sounds like a crossword clue."

"Never mind what it sounds like!" raged Elfish. "What about all those hours of research you said you did? You told me you couldn't find any more Mab poems apart from another one by Herrick and now Mo has replied to my Herrick with this poem by Shelley. Even I have heard of Shelley. It can't be that obscure. Did you do any research for me at all?"

"Hours of research," protested Aran. "Laborious, backbreaking, meticulous—"

Elfish cut him off, marching across the living room to take Aran's *Children's Wonderful Encyclopaedia* from the bookshelf. She practically ripped it open at "S" and scanned through it for Shelley.

"Aha!" she said with triumph. "What about this then? *Queen Mab.* Listed here as an early work by Shelley. In nine cantos, whatever that means. Well?"

"Even the most careful researcher can occasionally miss some obscure reference," said Aran.

"It's in your *Children's Encyclopaedia* for God's sake!" bawled Elfish. "For all I know it might be one of the best-known poems in the English language! Exactly how long did you spend in the library?"

Aran could only defend himself rather lamely while Elfish berated him. "Can I count on no help at all from anyone? Are you all completely useless?"

Eventually Aran was obliged to promise faithfully to find a new Queen Mab poem for his sister.

"No matter how strenuous an exercise it proves to be."

Elfish was placated, more or less.

"So did you make any progress with the speech?" asked Aran.

"Of course I didn't!" yelled Elfish, exploding again. "How am I meant to learn a speech when every time I turn round Mo and Cody annoy me by sending me another poem? Soon I'll be able to paper the walls with them. They are mocking me. Well, they won't get away with it."

Aran tried to make things up to his sister by helping her with the speech but their joint endeavours met with no success. Elfish in her state of tension could not remember a single line. Her best mental efforts were entirely in vain. Faced with impending disaster Elfish cursed and raged against the world. It was in fact so hopeless that Aran wondered if he should program Elfish into his computer game as she seemed to be fast becoming another person whose life had subsided into failure.

thirty

WALKING HOME FROM Aran's, Elfish was gloomy. She had a disturbingly clear picture in her mind. It was a vision of hundreds of Mo's friends and hundreds more of her enemies standing in front of the stage next Saturday, laughing at her.

It was time for resolute action but her experiences that day had left her too drained to take any kind of action at all.

I am defeated, she thought, struggling in through the front door.

I am never defeated, she thought, as she climbed the stairs. She picked up her Shakespeare once more. She read for several minutes before abandoning it.

I am still not defeated, Elfish told herself. But I'll do it tomorrow. She went to bed with her whisky bottle.

Her sleep was interrupted by the arrival of Aran around two A.M. He appeared to be badly shaken.

"What's happening?" mumbled Elfish.

"A terrible experience," said Aran, mopping his forehead. "I came with an idea for the backdrop you want."

Elfish blinked. Befuddled as she was by drink and sleep she was conscious enough to be surprised at her brother's unwarranted activity. Something about her band must be registering powerfully within him to bring him out of his home at this time of night. Unless of course he was just feeling guilty about his lack of research on her behalf.

"What idea?"

"But when I reached your house there were these two young people outside, holding hands—"

"Cary and Lilac," snorted Elfish. "They're always doing it."

"But that wasn't all. They had a handful of daisies and they were putting them in each other's hair."

Aran shook with painful emotion. Such a wanton display of love was even more ruinous to his fragile state of mind than it had been to Elfish's. Unable to say any more, he grabbed for Elfish's bottle of whisky and slid into bed beside her.

"It was awful," he muttered. "It shouldn't be allowed."

"There, there," said Elfish. "Don't worry, it'll pass."

"Don't they realise the harm they might do, hanging around in public putting daisies in each other's hair?"

Aran drank deeply, and rambled on for a while about how Cary and Lilac should be severely punished.

"Run them out of town, I say."

Elfish leaned forward to switch on the TV. Night-time programmes had begun and *American Gladiators,* one of her favourites, was on the screen.

With the alcohol, the TV and his sister's presence Aran began to make a slow recovery.

"What was that about a backdrop?" asked Elfish, during the adverts.

"The backdrop. I forget."

Aran searched his memory.

"Right. The backdrop. I know someone who can paint you one.

Aisha. When I was round her house she was painting something on canvas. She's a good artist. She'd do it."

Elfish considered this.

"She might. But Aisha is renowned for her personal problems. In an area full of sick people, she stands out. How do you know her?"

"I went to bed with her."

Elfish was reasonably impressed by this because Aisha had a regular boyfriend and was very beautiful. She asked her brother how it had happened.

"We were with some friends at a gay men's nightclub. I can't remember why we'd gone there. After dancing for a while she started kissing me. None of the gay men seemed to mind."

"I expect they'd seen worse."

"No doubt. The club had a fur-lined toilet."

"So what was it like in bed with her?"

Aran said he could not remember very well except Aisha had made a lot of noise.

"I mean really a lot, an abnormal amount of noise, practically screaming. I was slightly concerned in case the neighbours complained. Also she seemed to be having more fun than me. But I don't remember much more than that till I woke up the next morning. Aisha was still extremely beautiful, which quite impressed me, after a late and drunken night. No doubt I looked dreadful. When I went out the room to the toilet I noticed a postcard sticking through the letterbox. I read it. It was from her boyfriend Mory in Canada. I hid it under the rug in case she saw it and felt too guilty to fuck again. Then I made some tea and Aisha woke up and we had sex again. It would have been fine except in the morning, after fucking, Aisha had a severe panic attack and I had to get dressed quickly and leave. I know from experience that if someone asks you to leave because

they are having a panic attack it is no good hanging around trying
to make yourself useful, they just want you to go. I don't know why
it happened. Still, apart from that, it was fun."

"Will you see her again?"

"I don't expect so. The postcard said her boyfriend is coming
back soon so she'll be busy. I like Mory, he's a painter as well."

Elfish reached for the whisky bottle. "So did this make you feel
any better about splitting up with your girlfriend?"

Aran shook his head and said no, it had made him feel worse.
Elfish mused on Aran's suggestion.

"You might be right. Aisha might paint me a backdrop for Queen
Mab, and that would be a good thing to have."

They settled down to watch the rest of *American Gladiators* with
interest, making comments about their favourite gladiators and the
games they liked best. Their mutual favourite was the assault course
where each contestant had to flee through a barrage of tennis balls
fired by a gladiator from a huge gun, stopping off at various places
to fire back with weapons of their own.

"I wish I could do that," said Aran.

"Me too," said Elfish.

"I have eight different cigarette cards now."

"Really. Eight already? Well done."

As *American Gladiators* came to an end they drifted off to sleep
in a loose embrace.

Outside, Cary and Lilac were mildly disgruntled at their failure
to earn money washing windscreens. On arrival at their first prospective site they had found it already occupied by six people, all of
whom were larger than them and all of whom indicated a strong
desire for Cary and Lilac to disappear quickly. They had then walked
all the way down to the next major road junction at Vauxhall, usually

a fertile site for windscreen cleaners, and were pleased to find no one there. Unfortunately they soon discovered that this was because the police had moved them all on and they were forced to leave when a police van drew up and a constable gave them a warning.

What else could they do for money?

They had phoned up the agency for the Bronte School of English but they did not need any more people to hand out leaflets and after that they were stuck. Although they had no more ideas they were not disheartened.

"Something will turn up," said Lilac. "Tomorrow we should just walk around Brixton for a while. Probably we'll meet someone who'll offer us some work."

Cary and Lilac both shared some sort of optimistic new-age philosophy, the general gist of which was that things usually turned out all right if you just expected them to.

Their problems therefore settled, they carried on placing daisies in each other's hair.

thirty-one

Elfish had now entered the transcendental state of the dedicated stage diver and was immune to the effects of pain, fear or exhaustion. Repeated journeys through the air gave her the hallucinatory feeling that she could fly, and was touching the ground only when she felt like it. Her feet felt light as she climbed and her body was weightless as she floated through space.

Particularly extraordinary for Elfish was the general feeling of benevolence towards the world she now felt. A whole swaying array of young people in front of the stage whom Elfish would normally have held in absolute disesteem now seemed to her like a pleasant, even worthy gathering. It was with a sense of goodwill that she pounded down on to their heads.

When next on the stage she noticed someone waving and screaming at her. It was Amnesia. After diving she had worked her way slightly to the side of the crowd and now stood in the middle of a little space on her own. Elfish understood the message. She ran the whole width of the stage to build up momentum then took a powerful leap towards her companion. She soared through space in a great arc, headfirst towards the concrete around Amnesia's feet. Her friend caught her safely, as Elfish knew she would. They sprawled on to the hard floor together, laughing. Scrambling quickly to their feet, they looked around for anyone holding a drink, demanded some of the contents, then began to push and elbow their way back to the front.

thirty-two

ELFISH EXPLAINED HER frustrations to Shonen.

"I went round to visit May on the Tulse Hill estate and she didn't live there anymore because all the squatters on the estate have just been evicted. The council used PIOs to get them out quickly."

Shonen understood what this meant. PIO stood for "Prospective Intended Occupant" and was a legal order the council could obtain from a magistrate to save the time of preparing a court case for a normal eviction, which could take some months. With a PIO, no notice or formalities were necessary and the squatters could be evicted immediately.

For the council to be able to do this they were actually supposed to have tenants waiting to move into these flats but the council were not too bothered by legal technicalities like this. They had no hesitation in using PIOs and then boarding up the flats and leaving them vacant.

This was what had happened on the Tulse Hill estate and the flats now stood empty, barricaded behind bolted-on metal shutters.

"It's disgusting," said Elfish.

"Yes," agreed Shonen. "Now more people are homeless and there are even more empty flats."

What Elfish had actually meant was that it was disgusting that she could not find May when she wanted her, but she let it pass.

Shonen was genuinely troubled, though. In Brixton, as in all parts of London, the number of homeless people had been growing at an alarming rate; hopeless defeated people sitting in doorways, apparently without hopes or dreams. The sight of this was very distressing to her.

"What happened to May?"

"I tracked her down to Camberwell. She is living in the bus with four New Zealanders and three other Irish people till she finds another place to stay. I asked her about joining my band but she wasn't keen. She said she had too many things on her mind to play music. I would have just forgotten about it but I don't have time to hunt around for more people so I asked if she wanted to call round for a cup of tea. A cup of tea is quite an attractive prospect when you're living in an old bus.

"When she came I let her play my guitar and she's really good. She was hitting it like a madwoman. You'd have sworn there was a motorway pile-up going on in the corner of the room. So I must have her in the band."

This was not going to be easy because May was, as reported by Aran, severely depressed by her experiences in prison and was having great difficulty in managing her life. The sudden eviction had not helped and May had told Elfish that her continual inability to find anywhere secure to live in London had completely drained her spirit.

"Well, that's easily solved," Elfish had told her. "Chevon is moving out of here next week and you can have her room. You will be secure here."

At this, May's spirit had revived, and she had agreed to play guitar with Elfish.

"I didn't know Chevon was moving out," remarked Shonen.

"She isn't," said Elfish. "But May is not to know that. And I told

May that the reason Chevon is having to move is because we found out she'd been stealing money from the telephone box so she mustn't mention it to her as it's a very touchy subject."

"What'll happen when May finds out it's not true?"

Elfish shrugged. By that time the gig would be over. Elfish would have the name Queen Mab and May could live in a cardboard box under Waterloo Bridge as far as she was concerned.

In the meantime there was the problem of finding a guitar for May. She had lost hers some time ago during an eviction. Elfish, indefatigable, was now determined to get one for her.

"I saw one in the little secondhand music shop and it was good but I couldn't afford it. But I'll get it, I'll think of something. I will have a band by Saturday. Now, about this speech."

Elfish noticed that Shonen had left the room, and waited impatiently.

"Have a good vomit?" said Elfish as Shonen returned. Shonen lowered her eyes, unable to joke about it.

"The speech."

"Right. The speech."

"Yes."

"Well?"

"I'm not very good at teaching people things," said Shonen. "Excuse me."

She hurried out of the room. Elfish dug her fingernails into the palms of her hands and wished desperately that she knew anyone else in the whole world capable of teaching her how to learn forty-three lines of Shakespeare, because if she did she swore she would never pay a visit to this bundle of neuroses again.

thirty-three

ARAN HAD FINISHED reading Herodotus. Having already read Thucydides and Xenophon he was now a knowledgeable man when it came to Ancient Greek historians and he was armed with many long anecdotes about Athenians, Spartans and Persians. This was not necessarily good news for the rest of the world but Aran was always willing to try. When Elfish arrived he started right in with an account of the overthrow of Croesus, King of Lydia. Elfish immediately put up a strong defence, telling him that she had no time to listen to a tale about the overthrow of Croesus, King of Lydia, as she was visiting with the express purpose of learning her speech.

"It's a very good story."

"No doubt, but some other time. The gig is in five days. Even now Mo's band is practising and I must make some progress. Help me learn."

Aran was not enthralled with the prospect. He had not yet given up all hope of relating the story of Croesus, King of Lydia, and tried to reintroduce the subject, but his sister judiciously disengaged his attention from the ancient world by asking him about his cigarette card collection.

"How many do you have now?"

"Twelve. Well, I've got more than twelve, but lots of them are doubles. I have twelve different ones. I estimate that I will be able to claim my five pounds reward very soon. Do you want to see them?"

"Later. Now I want to learn the speech."

"Well, all right. Shakespeare it is. What is that smell?"

"Probably me," admitted Elfish. "After drinking all that whisky last night I wet myself. I'll have a bath later. Well, maybe. If I have time."

Elfish found it hard to focus her attention because she was currently working on another problem, that of Aisha. She had contacted the painter, confidently expecting to find her in her usual nervous and distressed state, in which she should be easily manipulable. Unfortunately for Elfish, Aisha seemed quite happy. Her boyfriend Mory had returned.

This was bad news for Elfish because not only was Aisha too happy to be easily manipulated, she was too busy working on a joint project with Mory to paint a backdrop. Unfortunately for Aisha, Elfish had now determined to have the backdrop and was already making plans.

thirty-four

AS A PASSENGER on the raft, Bomber Harris was no more cheerful than anyone else. He was depressed because so many people criticised him for destroying Dresden in an enormous bombing raid during the Second World War.

Opinion on the raft was divided. Pericles and Cleopatra thought that destroying an enemy city in wartime was an entirely sensible thing to do but Botticelli and Mick Ronson were unhappy about all the civilians who had been killed.

Here Aran intended to move his game into intellectual spheres by making the players become involved in a moral argument, but when he actually tried to do it it did not seem so easy. He sat grappling with the concept but after a few moments he found his attention wandering. Typing moral arguments into his terminal was frankly boring.

To hell with it, he thought, abandoning the idea, and sending in another squadron of screaming gryphons to harass the raft.

In the midst of the battle a new character appeared.

"I demand to know what I am doing on this raft," said Shonen, and vomited over the side, watched by an unsympathetic Pericles.

"How's the theatre group going?" asked Mick Ronson.

"Terribly," replied Shonen.

"Well, I guess that's what you're doing here."

Shonen thought for a moment.

"But Elfish is going to help me to be successful."

"That's what you think," muttered Aran, and laughed along with his scratchy tape of the Fall's "League Moon Monkey Mix."

This amused Aran for a while, programing in Shonen and Aisha as unwitting victims, but later he removed them in case Elfish found out and was annoyed. Elfish's short temper was always liable to be touched off by any small thing she did not like. She was not one of those people who could lightly laugh at themselves. In fact, thought Aran, growing slightly annoyed, Elfish takes herself entirely too seriously.

Had this thought of Aran's been generally known it might well have met with approval, but it would also have met with amusement because Aran himself was well known as a person who really did take himself too seriously: a blinding social affliction—no one can ever recognise it in themselves.

Elfish phoned, demanding to know if he had found a poem for her yet. Aran replied that he had not.

"I've been too depressed to visit the library."

"You mean you won't even visit a library to help your own sister when she is up against people so desperate as to shove poems by Shelley through her letterbox?"

Her brother gave in and agreed to go out and research although this was not something he wished to do. Whilst Aran might like to give the impression that he was quite at home in a library, surrounded by literature, he was really far happier at home playing video games and watching daytime television, and ogling the young female presenters.

Back onscreen Botticelli was struggling vainly with the rudder. Aran was not totally satisfied with his choice of Botticelli as an occupant of the raft.

"I don't think he is tragic enough," he had told Elfish. "Maybe I should have picked a painter that more bad things happened to."

"Well, why don't you?"

"I don't know much about any other painters."

"What about Van Gogh?" suggested Elfish. "He was really tragic."

Aran rejected this, claiming not to like Van Gogh because he was too modern and never painted the inside of a church. So he stuck with Botticelli. After all, game players were fairly dumb, as far as Aran could see. For all they knew, Botticelli might have been an immensely tragic figure.

thirty-five

JOHN MACKIE WONDERED if he should give up the struggle, close his shop and retire. He gazed without pleasure around the small confines of his premises. They were poorly lit, poorly stocked and bereft of customers.

Today as always he had attended ten o'clock Mass at St. Mary's Church, staying behind briefly to light a candle for his long-dead sister. The pain of her loss, stretching over fifty years, felt worse today. It had felt worse since the young woman who resembled her had come into his shop.

A small bell on the door rang as someone entered. John Mackie was not particularly pleased to see that it was the same young woman.

Elfish had walked down the street forcing herself to be cheerful, trying to lift her mood by an effort of will. She had again been overtaken by the feeling that this was all too difficult and she was never going to recruit a band and learn a speech in the required time. She was now lying to herself, quite consciously.

"It's easy," she said. "No problem. May just needs a little encouragement. Once she has her own guitar in her hands she will be pleased to be in my band. I'll just go and see that man in the music shop and make him a reasonable offer."

"Yes?" said John Mackie, and winced slightly as Elfish brushed her hair from her face and looked again like his sister, although his sister would never have had a stud and a ring through her nose.

"I would like that guitar," said Elfish. "And although I don't have enough money I will trade you this guitar for it, and pay off the balance."

Elfish held up a fairly mangy specimen of guitar. It was a cheap Gibson copy which was missing three strings. Two of its machine heads were badly bent and the controls and scratch plate were very much the worse for wear.

John Mackie shook his head. The guitar on offer was not worth as much as the one she wanted and although he would accept it as a deposit and allow Elfish to pay off the rest he would not allow her to take the new guitar away before the whole sum was paid.

"But I need it now. It is of great importance that my band get started right away. Otherwise I will not be able to use the name Queen Mab and you will naturally appreciate how important that is. It's also of great importance to my friend May that she have a guitar. Otherwise she may sink into such a mental state as to be unrecoverable. Besides, this is only the start of much business I'll put your way. So please give me the guitar and I promise to come in every week and pay it off."

John Mackie stared at her. He had not remained in business for so long by accepting such ridiculous offers as this. He was about to tell her abruptly to leave his shop when Elfish again swept back her hair, this time tucking the beaded fringes behind her ears, and proceeded to look even more like his sister. Her lip trembled. A tear formed in her eye and threatened to trickle down her cheek. John Mackie had the confused thought that he was somehow making his own sister cry. Unable to bear this he abruptly surrendered. Bemused by his own actions, the owner of the shop let her have the guitar, on the promise to pay for it later.

Marching down the street, Elfish was triumphant. She had learned from Shonen the actress how to start crying and make herself look pathetic and it seemed to have worked very well. The guitar was hers and would serve well for May. Now she had another member of her band, with equipment, and felt that she was well on her way.

Of course it had meant stealing Gail's guitar and trading it away and Gail was bound to be suspicious of Elfish but she would never be able to prove anything. Elfish had got up early that morning to remove the instrument and on leaving the house had cunningly left the door open. This would enable her to claim that they must have been burgled during the night. Possibly she could violently criticise Gail or Chevon for coming in from the pub drunk again and forgetting to shut the door. In reply to any enquiry as to her own movements she would use Aran as an alibi and claim to have spent the night at his flat. All in all it was an excellent morning's work.

Passing a charity shop, Elfish went in for a look around, hunting for more T-shirts and socks. As she wandered round she practised her speech.

> O! then, I see, Queen Mab hath been with you.
> She is the fairies' midwife, and she comes
> In shape no bigger than an agate-stone
> On the fore-finger of an alderman,
> Drawn with a team of little atomies . . .

Elfish could manage no more than five lines. How many lines did that leave? Being very poor at arithmetic she could not easily subtract five from forty-three in her head but it was definitely a lot. The pleasant glow from her good morning's work vanished quickly and a familiar gloom set in.

Elfish found some socks. Her motorbike boots had been feeling a little loose lately. Either they had expanded or her feet had lost weight. She paid for them and put them on immediately, stretching them over her numerous other pairs and then cramming her boots back on, now satisfactorily tight.

She took the guitar to May, returned home, abused the cat and got on with her Shakespeare. Gail was in tears about the loss of her guitar, which brightened Elfish's mood a little.

thirty-six

CARY AND LILAC were meanwhile continuing their career as Brixton's most hated couple. They held hands, wandered around, and looked for some source of income. Unfortunately there did not seem to be much income to be had, and after a great deal of wandering they found themselves back at their own house, sitting on the front wall.

Chevon and Perlita appeared with their bicycles. Cary and Lilac greeted them and were greeted in turn, although not with much enthusiasm. Elfish's four flatmates, though far less hostile to the world than her, still found Cary and Lilac hard to take now that their magazine had collapsed before even getting off the ground.

Along with Marion and Gail, Chevon and Perlita felt that they were now bereft of their main purpose in life and in these circumstances it is rarely pleasant to be unable to leave your house without meeting two people grinning inanely at you and telling you what a lovely day it is. Defeated by a lack of distribution, Chevon and Perlita felt that few days would qualify as lovely.

Distribution, they told each other, was a very effective manner of censorship. While there was no law to prevent them from writing or producing their magazine full of radical views, neither did there seem to be any way of getting these views across to others. And while no one could deny that the country was in a far worse state after years of rule by the Conservative Party than it had been before they came to power, no one any longer seemed to have any desire to do anything about it. The whole nation languished instead in front of TV sets and video machines.

Young radical feminists in Brixton also languished in front of TVs and video machines, but not all of the time. Some of them still tried to make their views heard, but it was very difficult.

Cody and Mo appeared, wearing leather and carrying guitars in cases. They had been rehearsing for the gig at the weekend and were returning to their own home which was on the far side of Elfish's.

Mo was reading a note with great displeasure.

An Almond parrat:
That's my Mab's voice,
I know by the sound.
—DEKKER

Cody had been fairly impressed when they received this, knowing that Dekker's *Westward Ho!* was not widely read these days, but Mo was simply annoyed.

"What the hell is an almond parrat? And how did I get involved in this in the first place? It's all your fault, Cody. You said Elfish would be dismayed when we gave her these obscure poems. Now she keeps giving us back even more obscure ones. I'm trying to run a rock band here, not judge a poetry contest."

But Mo could not give up on the subject because if he let Elfish have the last word he knew that she would use it as evidence of his alleged stupidity.

"You better deal with it, Cody. You'll have to find another one."

"Don't worry," said Cody, spotting Cary and Lilac. "I already have a good idea."

"Come inside," said Cody to the young couple. "I have a business proposition for you. I want you to pose for a picture of Queen Mab."

thirty-seven

ELFISH, WITH MUCH to do, had a late afternoon drink then felt too tired to carry on. Her drinking had been a problem for some time and now, when she most needed her wits and her energy, it was getting worse. She was becoming more and more frantic about her inability to learn the speech and this worsened every time someone stopped her in the street to ask her about it. Elfish had not bargained for Mo telling everyone and the scale of her impending humiliation left her terrified. It seemed that everyone in Brixton was going to be at the gig and they were all coming early to see Elfish recite Shakespeare.

Many of the people who asked Elfish how she was getting on pretended to be sympathetic to her cause but Elfish suspected that in reality they disliked her and were looking forward to her failing. In this supposition she was correct.

Depressed and unenthusiastic she found it hard indeed to summon up the energy to visit Aisha.

Only when a strong mental image of the hated Mo floated into her head did she manage to rouse herself and leave the house. She walked through the tiny part of Brixton which appeared to be thriving, with a new McDonald's, a Pizza Hut and a cinema about to be refurbished, much against the will of its patrons, and on along the street till the shops became smaller and grubbier and the pavements were strewn with rubbish.

Her way took her through the Loughborough estate, the first part of which was a truly dreadful collection of grubby white tower blocks separated by windswept and unfriendly patches of grass and concrete. Scaffolding stood around the entire reaches of one huge block. They were being repainted at the rate of one every two years, and young thieves were the main benefactors of this endeavour, using the scaffolding to creep easily into eighth-floor dwellings and burgle the flats, week after week.

Past this came the old red-brick blocks. The concrete that surrounded them also showed signs of refurbishment. Some government grant or other had arrived to spruce up the estate with newly painted railings and a children's playground, but vicious-looking dogs were the only occupants of the playground and behind every letterbox sat a council-tax demand that none of the occupants could pay.

Aisha lived here. Aisha was familiar to Elfish mainly from her brother's description of her, although she was well known generally as a woman who suffered from agoraphobia and panic attacks on a regular basis.

Let this go simply, thought Elfish, ringing the bell. I do not want to cope with anybody else's problems today.

"Go away," shouted Aisha through the door. "I'm having a panic attack."

Elfish scowled and bent down to the letterbox.

"Let me in, Aisha, I need your help."

"I can't see anybody, it's too severe," said Aisha.

"Well, it's not as fucking severe as it's going to be if I kick this door down!" screamed Elfish, losing all patience. She raised one large boot.

The door opened, revealing a shaking and trembling Aisha.

"Please go away," she said.

Elfish barged her way in.

"Put your panic attack to one side for the moment, Aisha. More important matters are afoot."

The guitarist strode confidently through to Aisha's main room. It was conspicuously clean and tidy due to Aisha's habit of doing housework to take her mind off her nerves. Elfish scanned the shelves and found what she was looking for, a bottle of vodka. She helped herself to a swig and shoved it into Aisha's hand.

"Calm down with this."

"I'm not meant to do that," protested Aisha. "The doctors—"

"To hell with the doctors. Take a drink."

She helped the shaky Aisha to drink some vodka. Aisha's trembling diminished very slightly.

"Well, now you're back to normal," said Elfish. "How about painting me a nice backdrop? Something suitable for a screaming thrash band with the excellent name of Queen Mab, deliverer of dreams."

"I can't."

"Why not?"

"I don't have any paint or materials. I don't even have a brush anymore. Mory took them all when he left me."

Elfish prepared herself to deal with another person's problems.

thirty-eight

WHEN ELFISH SAW Cary and Lilac sitting on their front wall she began to feel that really this was too much. They had a tape player beside them and they were listening to a very old recording of Marc Bolan in his hippie days.

> I could have danced,
> with my princess
> To the light of the magical moon.

They smiled at Elfish. She groaned. Returning home these days seemed like running a gauntlet, something on a par with smuggling guns to the Indians. Or, as her flatmates would undoubtedly inform her sharply, Native Americans.

"Hello, Elfish. Guess what?"

"I don't care what," rasped Elfish, beyond humour.

"We've got a job," Cary beamed.

"Cody is painting us. A scene from Jonson's *Queen Mab*, he says."

Elfish reeled as if assaulted, and turned on her heel abruptly, heading for Aran's.

"Mo and Cody have grossly insulted me again by picking Cary and Lilac as models for a new Queen Mab painting."

Elfish was completely, totally, overwhelmingly outraged by this. The picture had been meant to be of her and now it was to feature these two appalling youths who tormented her night and day by kissing in public and whispering secrets to each other.

"I should have attacked them," she raged, and made to leave. She stopped only when her brother waved a beer can at her.

"I don't suppose it matters really," he said.

"Of course it matters. Queen Mab is *my* name. It's not for all and sundry. Everyone can't go around being Queen Mab. It defeats the whole object. What's more, Mo is trying to show he knows more than me about Queen Mab again. He has countered my putting the Dekker poem through his door by this new action of finding a Ben Jonson play. Who is Ben Jonson incidentally?"

"He's on the raft in my video game," said Aran. "Haven't you noticed?"

"Well, who was he really?"

"A contemporary of Shakespeare. He was buried with the inscription 'Rare Ben Jonson,' so people at the time thought he was a good playwright, but really he was nothing like as good as Shakespeare. Entirely two-dimensional."

Here Aran was quoting the standard and rather old-fashioned view of Ben Jonson which he had read in a book. Along with the rest of his views on literature, it contained no original thought or insight.

Nonetheless, Aran was secretly impressed that Cary and Lilac were to be featured in a painting of Ben Jonson's "Entertainment," featuring Queen Mab, because this was a rather forgotten work, much more obscure than *Romeo and Juliet*, on which Elfish's Queen Mab portrait was to have been based.

"If you know enough about this person to program him into your video game, how come you didn't know he had written about Queen Mab as well?" said Elfish, with some justification. "Have you actually read anything he wrote?"

"Of course," replied Aran. "His entire works. Well, most of them anyway. There may be a few gaps here and there."

"Ha!" snorted Elfish. "I don't expect you ever read a play of his in your life. You probably just looked him up one time in your *Children's Encyclopaedia.*"

Aran changed the subject. Elfish departed. Again upset and pressurised she found herself unable to learn any lines, and the gig crept ever closer.

thirty-nine

ELFISH STOLE A black sheet from Chevon's bedroom to make a back-drop with, but a thorough search of the house revealed neither a paintbrush nor any paint. She needed several pounds to buy these for Aisha, so she borrowed a little money from Aran and begged for the rest in front of Brixton tube station.

Elfish was not humiliated by begging but she resented the time wasted, and it was hot. Summer seemed to be approaching fast and this always discomfited her. She disliked hot weather and regarded the sun as an enemy, particularly if it became so hot that she was obliged to discard her leather jacket. Without her jacket she never felt entirely secure.

Commuters flocked past her as the trains arrived but they generally ignored her, as they ignored the men selling cheap socks and handkerchiefs from upturned crates who kept a close watch for policemen, hastily packing up and moving if any came into view.

Across the pavement from Elfish was another man selling a tray of rings and beside him were three young men around a stall selling pamphlets about an organisation called the Nubian Nation. Beside them a young man and woman had laid out post-ers for sale on the pavement and beyond them was another beggar sitting cross-legged with a hat in front of him in which there were two small coins.

"Can you spare ten pence, please?" asked Elfish to all who passed. Few people wished to spare ten pence and it was slow progress.

She clutched her locket that contained the moonlight and mused on Aisha's tale of sex, her last adventure before her agoraphobia came on fully and her boyfriend Mory left her.

"I met two young Frenchmen at a modern motorbike circus," Aisha had told her. "They rode their bikes around the arena through fire hoops and stuff and they had leather jackets with metal bits sewn on, like yours, though not as good. In the arena they juggled and tossed fire clubs around, you know the sort of thing. I didn't really like it but I liked them when I met them in the bar afterwards.

"I went back with them to the place they were staying, a room in someone's house somewhere in Peckham. I was quite drunk and so were they and though I had imagined I might end up sleeping with one of them it hadn't occurred to me that I might end up sleeping with both of them together until they asked. Quite charmingly, I remember. I agreed because they both looked so cute in their leather and metal jackets. They were both about three years younger than me which seemed to make them cuter."

Aisha paused, and drew on her cigarette. She was a compulsive smoker.

"What happened when you went to bed?" asked Elfish.

"The place caught fire."

Elfish was impressed.

"Really? It was that good?"

"No, I mean the house actually did catch fire. I dropped a cigarette into some of the fuel they put on their fire clubs and it went up in a flash and we had to run out into the street. A terrible shame, though not as bad as it might have been because this was after we had finished having sex.

"You know, when we started I remember thinking that it might possibly be difficult working out which body to pay attention to but they made it easy for me by both licking me between my legs at the same time, which was an excellent sensation. I can't remember ever being more turned on. They both had these lithe acrobatic bodies with tight muscles and messy black hair and really a lot of earrings and they were licking my cunt practically inside out and licking my thighs and it was just great.

"After that I can't remember the precise sequence of events. I did straddle one of them and fuck him whilst sucking the other one. He came in my mouth and after that I sucked the other one's cock and I was fucking the other one at the same time or rather he was fucking me which was energetic, I thought, him fucking again so soon after coming. No doubt all these acrobatics kept him fit.

"All this activity in a warm bedroom made us sweat a lot and by this time we were practically sliding off each other's bodies. I remember having the distinct impression that there was a penis in every direction. Wishful thinking, I suppose. But the drink made me tired after coming myself and I needed a rest for a cigarette and that's when I set the house on fire. I just grabbed my clothes and fled. I never actually knew whose place it was I destroyed."

Aisha smiled.

"Excellent fuck. But when I arrived home without my shoes Mory was there unexpectedly and although I lied about where I'd been he knew that something had happened and he left me. I don't understand that bit of it. He'd never been suspicious of me before. I wonder if someone told him stories about what I'd been up to when he was away in Canada.

"Anyway, after that my agoraphobia came on worse and now I never go out if I can help it. Also I don't have any paint or even a brush and I don't think I could paint anymore even if I had. These days I spend most of my time being sad and missing Mory or having panic attacks."

Aisha slumped in deep depression. Elfish went out to beg.

"Can you spare ten pence, please?" said Elfish, and smiled in fake gratitude as a young man dropped some coins into her hand. Counting, she found that she now had enough and headed off to the cheap home-decorating shop down the road to buy materials.

Is everyone depressed? wondered Elfish, and decided that yes, they probably were. She did not care about everyone being depressed but resented the way it kept getting in the way of her plans. She wished that just one time she could ask someone to do something and they would rise enthusiastically, agree immediately, then go and do it. She did not really expect this ever to happen.

On the other hand, if Aisha had not been depressed it would have been because she was still with Mory, and in that case she would have been too busy working on their joint project to do anything for Elfish. So Elfish could only feel that she had been justified in privately informing Mory about Aisha's night in bed with Aran. The suspicion thus created had no doubt led to Mory not believing Aisha's cover story after she arrived home without any shoes from her night with the two acrobats and had therefore led to the collapse of their relationship. Very depressing for Aisha of course, but at least she was doing something useful now, that is, working for Elfish.

forty

IT TOOK ELFISH no thought or effort to lie to Aisha, telling her that she had been in contact with Mory by telephone.

"And he misses you dreadfully," Elfish informed her. "So you don't have anything to worry about. He's coming to the gig and he more or less told me he is going to ask you back."

Aisha was ecstatic at this, indeed she was about to phone Mory right away but Elfish hastily persuaded her that this would be a bad idea.

"You mustn't appear too eager. Make him wait a few days. After all, it was him that finished with you so he deserves to suffer a little. By the weekend he'll be desperate. Probably at the gig he'll march in and sweep you off your feet. Meanwhile, get on with painting the backdrop."

This was a cheering start to the day for Elfish but her mood quickly deteriorated. She tried learning some more lines of the speech but made no progress and a familiar melancholy settled in. When she found that not only could she learn no more, but that the few lines she had remembered had now entirely vanished from her mind, her mood deepened from melancholy to depression. After thinking about it for long enough, anxiety set in. She wondered if she might have caught this off Aisha, or Shonen. Perhaps anxiety was contagious, like measles.

Today she was meant to be visiting Shonen for more help with the speech but Elfish feared that whatever Shonen did it would not help her to get beyond line three. She found herself wondering why she had ever become involved in anything as ridiculous as this contest. Mo merely wished to humiliate her by showing her to his friends as a woman so desperate for something she was prepared to try and learn an impossible speech from Shakespeare, and so hopeless that she could not do it. She cursed her brother for suggesting it, and cursed Mo for everything.

Elfish's mouth was rank and foul from cigarettes and alcohol. The taste was sickeningly bad. She had a great resistance towards brushing her teeth, possibly connected to dim memories of her parents instructing her to do it regularly. At this moment she would not have been able to say when she had last cleaned them.

Elfish's circumstances were actually worse than she thought they were, because at that moment Mo was waking up contentedly with Amnesia.

"Do you think Amnesia will phone today?" he asked, and they both laughed.

When Elfish had phoned up yesterday, pretending to be Amnesia, Amnesia had sat next to Mo at the phone and it was all she could do to stop herself from screaming with laughter. She thanked the good fortune which had brought her back into Brixton and into the path of Mo at this very moment. Ever since her last day's stage diving with her ex-friend, Amnesia had waited and wondered how she could repay Elfish for her badness.

Mo was now aware that Elfish was plotting against him. He could not work out the precise nature of her machinations but it seemed clear that she must believe herself to have an advantage. Thinking back to his conversations with her when she had been pretending to be Amnesia he could recall how she had carefully manoeuvred him into a position whereby he agreed to give up the name of Queen Mab if Elfish learned the speech and produced a band. He still found it hard to believe that Elfish could do either of these things in so short a time but Elfish must at least be confident that she could. Mo did not intend to be defeated by Elfish. Nor did he intend to cede the name to her. With a view to frustrating Elfish he asked his friends and contacts to talk to people and find out exactly what she was up to.

forty-one

The gig was nearing its climax. Elfish and Amnesia still swooped around like crazed eagles. In the morning Elfish would be a mass of bruises and abrasions but at this moment she was immune to all discomfort.

For the hundredth time Elfish was fighting her way back to the stage. She paused near two boys who still had cans of beer in their hands.

"Give me a drink," said Elfish.

"No," they replied.

Elfish would often ask strangers for drinks at gigs and was used to refusals so she would have thought nothing of this had not Amnesia at that moment appeared beside her.

"Give me a drink," she said to the two boys.

Immediately they both handed over their cans to her and she drank from them. She offered one to Elfish. Elfish took it but her eyes were narrowed and she assumed that the boys had given Amnesia their drinks merely because she had long blonde hair. Elfish was used to this and shrugged it off. She continued on her way, digging her elbows into those around her to make her way once more up on to the stage.

The bouncers had by this time more or less given up and Elfish had an easy ascent. Once onstage, she kicked the lead singer's microphone stand over for fun then jumped mightily into the air. Elfish leapt in no particular direction but her keenness for this last jump carried her far and she crashed down close to the vacant space at the side of the stage. Only one person stood there and Elfish was fortunate to land on him rather than the concrete.

They both stood up and the person moved away, possibly feeling that this place was no longer safe. As Elfish looked up she saw that Amnesia was now onstage, preparing to jump. Amnesia saw her, waved, sprinted a few yards to the side of the stage and leapt directly at Elfish, intending to land on her, just as Elfish had previously landed on Amnesia in the same spot.

But Amnesia did not land on Elfish. As she sailed through the air Elfish stepped quickly to one side and the gap thus created was just large enough for Amnesia to crash headfirst on to the concrete where she lay without moving.

She was helped away backstage and later in hospital it was found that her collarbone was broken and she was concussed. She was obliged to remain in hospital for several days.

Afterwards Elfish and Amnesia never spoke. There seemed little to say. Amnesia knew that Elfish had deliberately moved out of the way, and Elfish knew that she knew. Once recovered, Amnesia retired from the area, going to live in the suburbs for a while until her shoulder healed. While in the suburbs she thought often about Elfish, and always with great animosity. Elfish's behaviour had been treachery of the worst kind, a wretched betrayal of a friend and fellow stage diver.

"Why did you do it?" asked Aran later, but Elfish was unable to supply a satisfactory answer so did not try. It might have been pique at Amnesia jumping farther than her, or it might have been annoy-

ance that she kept landing on Mo and that Mo seemed to respond to her favourably. Or it might have been jealousy that the boys had refused drink to Elfish but supplied it to Amnesia.

It might have been none of these things. Elfish could not really say. When Amnesia was hurling towards her, she just felt like moving out of the way, and she could never honestly say that she felt very sorry about it.

forty-two

THOUGH SHONEN'S BULIMIA had improved after Elfish's encouraging news about the fund-raiser, it was a long way from being cured. Today she had been shopping in the supermarket and this had been a stressful experience from start to finish. Touring around the shelves pushing a trolley she experienced both the irresistible urge to stock up with some junk food and the certain knowledge that once she had eaten it she would feel bad and throw it all up again.

Driven by whatever childhood misery fuelled her disorder, she swept supplies into the trolley. As she did so, she practised excuses and reasonable stories in case anyone asked her why she was buying so much food; Shonen's guilt about eating extended to a paranoia that other people knew all about it and were watching with disapproval.

"I have a large family to feed," she would say, if challenged by the checkout woman. "I rarely get the chance to shop; I am buying provisions for a month. The woman next door to me fell down and broke her leg and I'm shopping for her as a favour. I am having a dinner party for twelve people and they are all big eaters."

Unchallenged by the checkout woman, or the manager, or the store detectives, she bundled her food into a collection of flimsy carrier bags and struggled home. She was so encumbered with food that on the outskirts of her estate it took her much time and effort to find her purse to give a little money to a hopeless-looking woman with no place to go who sat begging beside the children's playground. Shonen always gave money to beggars.

Once home she wolfed down a meal, vomited, ate, vomited, ate, vomited, then collapsed. She was on the verge of plunging into total despair when she remembered that things were not entirely without hope. Elfish was coming to the rescue. Elfish was going to put her theatre group back on the rails. These days the thought of Elfish had become very inspiring, looming large over Shonen's hopelessness like a benevolent goddess.

Shonen cleaned up the toilet, resisted the urge to eat again, and forced her bulimia from her mind. With an effort of will she made herself think positively about a new production. This was such a pleasant thing to contemplate that not long afterwards she was on the phone to the rest of her group, practically bullying them out of their own defeatism with enthusiastic plans for the future.

Despite being neurotic, depressed and defeated by life, Shonen was not one of Brixton's lonely characters. She had many friends and was frequently in contact with the various members of her theatre group.

These fellow performers were surprised by the sudden change in her. She had organised their appeals for funding and sponsorship and now called them up to organise planning meetings for a new season. She invited them round for drinks and launched into enthusiastic discussions about writing and rehearsing a new play and taking it to next year's Edinburgh Festival. And, she said, if the Edinburgh Festival did not work out then they could do it free in a pub somewhere. Anything to perform.

When the members of the acting group asked her what had brought about this abrupt change in her demeanour, this sudden enthusiasm for life quite uncharacteristic of her recent behaviour, Shonen unhesitatingly gave all of the credit to Elfish. Elfish had taken the trouble to find someone who could actually help them and she appreciated this immensely. Not only that, Elfish's strident endeavours to bring her own ambitions to fruition had acted as a powerful inspiration to Shonen.

"If she can overcome her difficulties, then so can we," she told her theatre group.

"Elfish is so determined. She is inspiring. If she says she can find us someone to look after our funding then she'll do it because Elfish does not give up."

Mo was at this moment thinking much the same thing, although not with kindness. He had learned from Irene Tarisa that Shonen was helping Elfish with her speech, and that May and Casaubon were playing in her band. Aisha was even painting a backdrop for her, which seemed like a sure sign that Elfish was confident of success.

Mo was perturbed, so perturbed that he spoiled his band's rehearsal that day by continually picking faults in each musician's contribution till the rehearsal ground to a halt in animosity and bad-tempered recriminations.

forty-three

ARTEMISIA WAS QUEEN of Halicarnassus in Asia Minor. She sailed with Xerxes, King of Persia, against the Greeks in 480 B.C. She was unique, being the only woman to fight in the war, a war which involved millions of men. She did not have to do this. Her husband had died, passing the sovereignty to her, but she had a grown-up son who could have led her forces. Artemisia was moved by the spirit of adventure.

Herodotus gives a very favourable account of Artemisia, possibly because he too came from Halicarnassus. Artemisia led a small squadron of ships, captaining the flagship herself, and gained a reputation for her prowess in war. The Greeks particularly hated the fact that a woman was fighting against them and offered a large reward for her capture but she was never taken.

Artemisia also gained a reputation as a shrewd adviser to the King. She was the only one of Xerxes's counsellors who advised him against fighting the battle of Salamis, saying that the huge Persian army should continue the war on land rather than sea. Xerxes did not take her advice and went on to suffer a catastrophic defeat at Salamis. His fleet was routed and his entire plan to conquer Greece suffered a severe setback. This increased Artemisia's reputation because her advice was proved to have been correct and Xerxes realised he should have paid heed to it.

Another event occurred during the battle which further increased her reputation. The vast Persian fleet, being outfought and outmanoeuvred by the superior Greek navy, was in full retreat. Artemisia's ship was fleeing along with the rest and she found herself hemmed in between a Greek pursuer and a ship of her own fleet which was blocking her retreat. Without hesitation Artemisia rammed this ship even though it was on her side. It sank with all hands. Her Greek pursuer, seeing this, presumed that Artemisia's ship must in fact be on his side and ceased the pursuit, allowing Artemisia to escape.

Xerxes was watching the battle from a hill near the shore.

"Do you see how well Artemisia is fighting?" said one of his advisers. "She has just sunk an enemy ship."

Xerxes, distressed about the destruction of his fleet, at least had one thing to be glad about, and made a comment which was to become well known. "What has happened to my army? The men have turned into women and the women have turned into men."

He later entrusted Queen Artemisia with the safe conduct of his children back to their home, which was a task of great importance and some danger.

Artemisia's immediate descendants built the Mausoleum, a famous building in Antiquity, parts of which can still be seen in the British Museum. "It's my favourite story from Herodotus," said Aran. "Would you like to hear my favourite story from Thucydides?"

"No," replied Elfish. "You know I can only listen to one story at a time."

"Very well," said Aran. "I'm going to put Artemisia into my video game. Would you like to play my video game?"

"Absolutely not. I detest your video game. Help me with the speech."

forty-four

ELFISH'S TWO REMAINING friends and pool partners, Tula and Lizzy, were also friends of May's. Not as close friends as they were of Elfish, but they had visited May during a trip to Ireland last year and she had received them very hospitably.

They were therefore pleased to learn from May that Elfish was finally providing her with a secure home in England.

"Secure for a while anyway," said Lizzy, as they sat waiting their turn on the pool table. "Although I see the government is bringing in a law making it illegal to squat."

This was to happen soon. In Brixton, a council flat would be just about affordable to rent but these were no longer given to single people, only to families, if they were fortunate. A private flat was so far out of the reach of most people it was not worth thinking about. Even an unpleasant bedsit was beyond the range of many people unless they could manage to have the rent paid by the social security, but this was hard to organise, and anyway landlords always wanted a deposit and a month's rent in advance so this was more or less out of the question as well.

This left squatting, and as the council had many unused flats it seemed like a sensible solution. The government, however, had now resolved to make squatting, the one remaining safety valve, illegal, and turn even more people out on to the streets.

A strong article by Chevon in her prospective newspaper had pointed out that this was very bad timing. The streets of London were already fully occupied. Homeless people were everywhere, as were beggars.

Distressingly, in recent years, these people had become far more lost and hopeless-looking than before, due to the government's triumphant new policy of emptying and closing mental institutions, moving the occupants from these institutions out into the community. Whether or not the actual intention of this "Care in the Community" policy was that the mentally ill should now be slumped in hopeless and degraded poverty in shop doorways everywhere was not clear, but this was certainly the effect. Many of the beggars who now held out their hands in Brixton were people who were clearly unwell and obviously unable to look after themselves. Some of them were not even able to hold out their hands. They just sat in silence on the pavements, and might sit there till they died. A few would shout and run about wildly. Who was now meant to be looking after these people, nobody knew.

Those who, despite being poor, displayed strong mental health by finding an empty place and squatting in it were now to be turned out to join in the throng.

Already there were fewer squats in Brixton; soon there would be none, and a small epoch would have ended. As the people involved were not very important the question of where they were actually meant to live was not one that anyone had bothered answering.

May, however, would be secure in Elfish's house, at least for a while.

"Where is Chevon moving to?" asked Lizzy.

"She isn't moving," Elfish told her frankly, but in this she made a bad misjudgement. She presumed that Tula and Lizzy would see immediately that it was a worthwhile deception in order to get May playing guitar on Saturday. They did not. They were outraged that Elfish was building up May's hopes falsely.

"May is in a really bad way," protested Lizzy. "When she finds out you've lied to her and there is no place for her to live she'll collapse completely."

Elfish, too obsessed to see the danger, merely shrugged. Tula and Lizzy were upset. They gathered up their leather jackets and left after lecturing Elfish briefly on what they saw as appalling behaviour.

Thus Elfish's last remaining friends walked out of her life, leaving her with only a depressed brother and a band of people she had lied to for her own purposes.

"Well, fuck them," muttered Elfish, and proceeded to wipe out her next opponent on the pool table, putting five balls down from her first break and finishing the game off on her next visit to the table.

In the pub people looked surreptitiously at her as she played.

"That is Elfish," whispered one person to another. "The woman who is so obsessed with naming her band Queen Mab that she is going to recite forty-three lines of Shakespeare on stage before Mo's gig on Saturday."

Everyone who knew Elfish informed everyone who did not that it seemed very unlikely that she could manage it, and interest in the whole proceedings continued to grow at an alarming rate. Complete strangers would stop Elfish to ask her about it. Unable to think quite what to say, Elfish would merely grunt at them. If they persisted with their questioning she would tell them brusquely to mind their own business. This was enough to silence most people but Elfish's aggressive manner made no impression on Mo and his friends. They laughed at her quite openly. Elfish no longer felt entirely comfortable in this pub although she had been coming here for some years. There were too many people whom she suspected of mocking her and looking forward to her downfall.

She would not stop coming though, even though it might mean standing by herself now that Tula and Lizzy would no longer come drinking with her. To abandon her usual haunts would mean accepting a defeat, which she would not do.

It was not pleasant drinking on her own, however. Even Aran would be some company but he would not come with her to this bar. As well as being too depressed to leave the house, he was worried that he might run into his old girlfriend, an event which he said would be too much for him to cope with.

forty-five

JOHN MACKIE SAT alone in his shop. There were no customers. He was watching a small television which rested on a chair behind the counter. Business was still bad but he was rather more cheerful than he had been.

This was due to Elfish. In the past few days she and May had been calling in constantly for leads, plectrums, a tuner, two fuzz-boxes, a microphone, a sustain pedal and various other bits and pieces they needed for their band. Everything they bought was the cheapest there was and even then part of the cost had to be put on to Elfish's bill but John Mackie found that he did not mind. He had become infected with Elfish's enthusiasm. It felt good that a woman who reminded him of his sister was coming into his shop, talking about her plans and generally being positive. Her visits gave him something to look forward to. Extending her credit was undoubt-edly poor business practice, but as things were so bad it made little difference and it brought him pleasure.

When she called in they would talk about what she required for the gig at the weekend and though he was not fully conversant with Elfish's overwhelming need to call her band Queen Mab, John Mackie was aware of the gig's importance to Elfish. He was willing to do what he could to help. The enthusiasm that this generated inside him was the first that he could remember for many years. Arriving at his shop that morning he had felt positively cheerful as he gave a little money to the homeless beggar who huddled in his doorway. The pavement outside John Mackie's shop was a popular place for homeless beggars. John Mackie took his Christian charity seriously, and was sorry for them, and gave them money.

The television news switched to a report from Sudan.

"Here the famine is becoming more serious every day," said a reporter, as the screen showed bodies thin beyond belief stumbling hopelessly in search of nourishment.

These pictures troubled him, and he resolved to donate money tomorrow to the famine relief fund at his church.

Aisha was watching the same programme while she painted the backdrop. "How terrible," she said, but what she really thought was, they could all die if only my boyfriend Mory would come back, and she carried on painting to block it out of her memory.

Aran too was watching the news.

"How terrible," he muttered, but what he really thought was much the same as Aisha. He switched off the TV and studied his cigarette cards to take his mind off his ex-girlfriend.

He frowned. Despite buying and smoking an immense amount of cigarettes he had not yet collected all twenty cards. He was stuck on eighteen. He had more than one of each of these. Of some of them he had as many as four. Yet his collection contained not a single example of either number three or number twenty.

"There is definitely something funny going on here," he mumbled. "I don't believe the company is distributing the cards fairly."

Various schemes whereby the cigarette company could cheat its customers and deny them their five pounds' reward floated through his head. There might not be any cards numbered three and twenty. This was a diabolical thought and brought Aran close to despair.

Musing further on this, though, he rejected it eventually as too risky for the company. If they did not print up any of one card then someone might notice. A disgruntled employee might talk to the newspapers. Word would leak out and the Serious Fraud Office would investigate. Altogether too dangerous for the board of directors.

They might, of course, only print up a tiny number of certain cards. It could be that there was only one number three in the whole country and it had been sent to Glasgow. That seemed quite likely, and Aran again felt desolate. Even more fiendishly, the company might be printing up an equal number of each card but ensuring the cigarette packets containing certain cards were sent only to carefully controlled locations. Every single card number twenty might at this minute be in a warehouse on the Orkney Islands, awaiting distribution to only one local tobacconist. Orkney Islanders, smoking away keenly to claim their reward, might find that every card in their collection was number twenty. And what legal redress would a person in London have against the company? None whatsoever. They did not say anywhere in their advertising that the cards were sent evenly around the country. Aran could now see clearly that the whole thing was a plot, fixed from start to finish.

"It's no use," he sighed. "These companies are too powerful. There is no way of winning against them."

Elfish appeared, looking extremely dirty and demanding a poem. To her surprise, Aran had one ready.

"From Milton's 'L'Allegro,'" he told her. "Have I ever told you the story of Milton's life? He was—"

"Shut up and give me the poem," ordered Elfish, and held out her hand.

Till the livelong daylight fail,
Then to the spicy nut-brown ale,
With stories told of many a feat;
How fairy Mab the junkets eat;

"What's a junket?" asked Elfish. "Never mind, don't tell me. This is fine. It will do to counter the painting of Ben Jonson's Mab. I'll go and put it through Mo's door right away."

forty-six

THE STORM ABATED but there was no respite for the exhausted occupants of the raft. The edge of the world was now in clear sight and the noise of the ocean falling away into the void rolled over them like thunder. With their situation growing ever more hopeless they began to bicker.

"Haven't you fixed the rudder yet?" complained Cleopatra.

"I'm doing my best," retorted Botticelli sharply.

"Well, it doesn't seem to be having much effect."

"I'm a painter, not an engineer."

"I'm sure Leonardo could have done a better job," said Cleopatra.

"So who are you to criticise?" demanded Botticelli. "All you do is strut around giving orders. I haven't seen you actually working yet. And this from a woman who lost a whole empire just because she picked the wrong Roman."

"Mark Antony was not the wrong Roman," retorted Cleopatra. "We were just unfortunate to lose the battle of Actium."

Bomber Harris, interested in this, started a conversation about wartime tactics through the ages but he was interrupted by Red Sonja.

"Shut up and keep working. It won't be long till the gryphons come back."

"Don't you tell me to shut up, you ignorant barbarian. I didn't notice you having any notable success when you tried to mend the sail."

"Stop bickering," said Ben Jonson, who was trying to nail the mast together. "We'll only get out of this situation if we all work together."

He looked pointedly at Mick Ronson, who still sat idly in the middle of the raft.

"I refuse to work any more," said the musician. "There's no point. We can't win. I'm going over the edge of the world strumming my guitar."

He launched into the solo from "Moonage Daydream," a song he had recorded while playing with David Bowie in 1972. This solo was full of long, high, lingering notes, building upon each other to beautiful effect.

"Ship ahoy!" screamed Cleopatra, and everybody looked in alarm, assuming it was some new enemy come to torment them.

"I recognise that ship," cried Pericles, great statesman of Athens. "It's Queen Artemisia."

He drew his sword, preparing to repel boarders, but it soon became clear that Artemisia was not going to attack. Her ship sailed on by, back towards the far distant shore.

Aran was programming the task for the next level. The raft had to somehow attach itself to Queen Artemisia's trireme. If they could do this they would be towed all the way back to safety. When the occupants of the raft realised this they made frantic efforts to make ropes from whatever material they had available, fixing Red Sonja's sword to the end as a grappling hook. They paddled frantically after the ship while Sonja prepared to cast the line.

Naturally it was hopeless. There was no way for the raft actually to come close enough to make the connection.

"You Failed," said the caption on the screen, after Sonja's repeated attempts to reach Artemisia's ship with her grappling hook all fell short. "You are now plunged into the next level, right at the Edge of the World."

forty-seven

MO'S LONG HAIR lay over his face and the carpet and Shonen sat over Mo, fucking him by the light of the television. She did this quite slowly. Her movements were noticeably more relaxed than normal.

Mo, who had been drinking, lay passively for a long time as Shonen rocked back and forth on top of him.

After a while he seemed to gather up his energy and reached up to take hold of her small breasts before dragging his body into a sitting position so that Shonen was kneeling on his lap and they kissed.

Mo had had no hesitation in asking Shonen to sleep with him towards the end of his first visit. Shonen had agreed because although she rarely had sex and thought about it seldom, there was something about Mo which she found attractive. Possibly it was the fact that he did not really care if she was alive or dead. More than one person had found that attractive about Mo, including Elfish. Another attraction was that he would leave immediately afterwards without bothering her for details of her personal life.

Shonen slid her hand between their bodies to grip Mo's penis lightly between two fingers as it entered her. Mo wrapped his arms round Shonen and slid his finger up her anus. Locked together, they rocked gently backwards and forwards in the dim light of the television.

When Mo was close to orgasm he brusquely shoved Shonen off his lap and on to her back and fucked her as hard as he could till he came, then lay momentarily on top of her, dripping with sweat.

He left soon afterwards. Shonen had not come, which was frustrating. Then again, sex had taken up more than an hour during which time she had had no desire to eat or vomit.

Later, however, she felt anxious lest Elfish should find out she had been having sex with Mo. Shonen knew that Elfish would not like this and she did not want to offend her.

Elfish was in her thoughts because Mo had questioned her about Elfish's progress with the speech. He had intimated that Shonen was unwise to help her. Shonen had explained to Mo that Elfish was doing her a favour in return although when she explained what it was Mo snorted and said that Elfish was certainly lying because no theatrical fund-raiser lived anywhere near her and anyway Elfish was a born liar.

Shonen did not believe Mo. She trusted in Elfish's efforts to aid her. Her physical theatre group was too important for her not to believe in Elfish. Even as Mo's semen was still trickling out of her body she was back at her sponsorship documents, and giving some thought to their next production.

For his part Mo had gained the impression that Elfish was close to success. He resolved to do something about it.

forty-eight

THE PROJECTED GIG was on Saturday and by Wednesday Elfish was
an ugly sight. Unwashed for a long time, a time which included not
enough sleep and too much to drink, her face was grimy, her body
stank, her clothes stuck to her frame and her hair was dusty in front
of her eyes.

As an aid to learning the speech Shonen had drawn it up for her
in different-coloured inks, hoping in this way to make Elfish word
associate with the different colours. She had made some progress
and was now on line fifteen:

Her chariot is an empty hazelnut

It was an immense effort. It seemed like the hardest thing she had
ever done.

Wearying of it, Elfish dropped the speech on the floor and picked
up her guitar. She plugged it into the amplifier. No sound emerged.
This was not unusual. With the cheap equipment Elfish used it was
a rare occasion when her guitar worked first time.

She fiddled with the lead till it came to life with a small crackle,
kicked her fuzzbox on and played to herself, not caring that the

noise would disturb the rest of the household. Tomorrow she would go back to the shop and beg for some better guitar leads.

Elfish was a good guitarist, somewhat more talented than most of her peers in the area. Although she liked to thrash her guitar viciously on stage she was also capable of playing some blues, or finger-picking a little country, or strumming a few jazz chords. She could even set up and maintain an African rhythm, learned through copying African records she heard on the radio, generally on John Peel. These African guitar songs danced along with skill and clarity and were full of life. Elfish hated them but copied the riffs for practice.

She took stock of her situation. Casaubon was playing drums, May was playing guitar, Shonen was teaching her the speech and Aisha was painting a backdrop. All she had to do was learn the speech, find a bassist, walk on stage and the name of Queen Mab would be hers.

Looked at this way things did not seem too bad and Elfish's confidence rose. She would triumph. She would defeat Mo although defeating Mo was not her main purpose. It was only a necessary step on the way to achieving her ambitions. Had it suited her ambitions to cooperate with him, she would have done so.

The gig would be terrible, of course. Not even Elfish expected that four poorly rehearsed musicians playing on stage together for the first time would be anything but dreadful, but this did not matter. In her present surge of confidence Elfish felt no fear of other people. If the crowd abused her she would happily abuse them back. Once the gig was over she would have time to make things work properly.

Feelings of confidence unfortunately did not allow Elfish to relax. She had too much to do. Also, the situation in her house had worsened. The other four women, depressed about their magazine, were now irritated beyond measure by Elfish's increasingly antisocial behaviour. They had asked her in the strongest terms to please leave the house. Elfish had refused and abused them roundly in return but she was now almost obliged to spend most of her time in her room.

She smoked cigarette after cigarette and played her guitar till her fingers were sore. Tomorrow she was meeting the others for a rehearsal and she had to have at least some idea of what she wanted them to play even though they would undoubtedly get it all wrong.

forty-nine

CARY AND LILAC sat in Cody's room, modelling for his painting of Ben Jonson's "Entertainment" play. Cody was painting Lilac as the Satyr and Cary as Queen Mab. In the background would be Queen Anne and her attendants.

The work in question went by the title of "A Particular Entertainment of the Queen and Prince," and had been written by Ben Jonson for a performance before Anne, Queen of James I of England and James VI of Scotland, in the grounds of Althrope, the Spencers' country mansion. It had been performed on June 25,1603, and first published in 1616. It was a short work of only one act.

Cody, not himself averse to showing off a little knowledge, related this to Cary and Lilac as they modelled for him. They smiled politely in return. Although he had completed only one year at art college before being ejected with ignominy, Cody still enjoyed his art. He had less time for it now he was playing guitar with Mo but he still painted regularly.

His style was positively old-fashioned. His paintings would never be shown in the alternative art gallery in Brixton, although according to Cody they would apparently show anything by anyone capable of throwing paint at a piece of canvas. If something other than paint was involved—rags, metal or unidentifiable debris—so much the better.

Although not nearly as dull and pedantic as Aran, Cody did occasionally cause Mo distress in a manner similar to the way in which Aran distressed Elfish. For instance, he likened Mo and Amnesia's campaign against Elfish to the great revenge tragedies of the sixteenth century, and even to those of the Roman dramatist Seneca, doing this while Mo was waiting at the bar for his pint and unable to flee.

This was just the sort of comparison Aran would have enjoyed, and had circumstances been different, he and Cody could have sat for hours discussing such things while Mo and Elfish drank and played pool together and talked about ways of getting in free to whatever violent gig they wanted to see next. Unfortunately the hostility that existed between Elfish and Mo did not allow Aran and Cody to be friends.

When Cody was casting around for models it had been Amnesia's idea that he ask Cary and Lilac, purely for the purpose of upsetting Elfish, in which they had succeeded. Amnesia now sat quietly in the next room, reading a book. She seldom left Mo's flat, wishing for the meantime to keep out of Elfish's sight.

Cary and Lilac sat quietly for the painting but, unusually, they were far from satisfied. Yesterday they had travelled down in a bus—the same bus in which May was living—to Twyford Down, an area close to Winchester. Twyford Down was a lovely and scenic place. It was officially designated as an Area of Outstanding Natural Beauty. As well as being beautiful, it was of archaeological importance, having been continually inhabited since before the Iron Age, and it contained two protected ancient monuments. Several rare species of wildlife, also protected, lived there. All in all it was a unique and precious site. The Department of Transport had now decided to build a motorway through it.

There had been protests about this for some time now and Cary and Lilac, friends of several people who had been there before, journeyed down with them to join in. It had not been a pleasant experience. The area was heavily policed and the work was already well under way despite the protests. The previously beautiful area was now scarred and disfigured by deep gorges. Large areas had been stripped of trees and grass. It was obvious that Twyford Down was not going to be saved, and the protected species of wildlife were just going to have to get used to living on concrete.

"They say that Camelot was on Twyford Down," said Lilac, and Cary shook her head sadly.

Cody asked her please to remain still while he painted her. He was grappling with the difficult task of reproducing her white dreadlocks. Perhaps this painting was not entirely traditional after all, but the white dreadlocks would look good on Queen Mab. Cody still regretted that he could no longer use Elfish as the model for the Queen of Dreams because he knew that her spirit had been right for the part.

While in this house Cary and Lilac heard much virulent abuse of Elfish. They regretted this because although Elfish was continually unpleasant to them, they liked her. For some reason they did not really believe that Elfish did not like them, in spite of all the virulent abuse she had thrown in their direction.

fifty

SHARING A BED, Aran and Elfish woke up together.

"I'm too unhappy about my girlfriend to carry on living," said Aran.

"Then go and pick up my new guitar leads from the music shop," said Elfish. "Doing something will make you feel better."

Elfish phoned Casaubon.

"I'm too unhappy about my girlfriend to carry on living," he said.

"Practise your drumming. Then go and get May and make sure she's ready to rehearse," said Elfish. "Doing something will make you feel better."

Elfish phoned Shonen.

"I'm too unhappy about everything to carry on living," said Shonen.

"Then get busy with your pile of papers for funding so you're ready for my neighbour to help you," said Elfish. "I'll be down soon. Doing something will make you feel better."

What a sad bunch, thought Elfish, leaving Aran's house.

"Hello, Elfish," said Cary and Lilac, who were perched cheerfully on the low wall outside. They tried to tell her about their experiences on Twyford Down but Elfish was not interested in this, not caring one way or the other if every beautiful spot in the country was concreted over. She was also upset at them for posing for Cody's Queen Mab picture. She felt that this was disloyal to her even though Elfish had never given Cary and Lilac any reason whatsoever to show her any loyalty.

"Haven't I told you never to speak to me again?" she snapped, and strode past with her eyes fixed firmly on her motorbike boots. For want of polish the leather was beginning to split, which was annoying, but cleaning boots was well outside Elfish's range of activities these days.

Stopping only to push the verse by Milton through Mo's letterbox, Elfish hurried down to Shonen's. Shonen received Elfish nervously though to Elfish this seemed perfectly normal. The actress was anxious after her encounter with Mo because although she did not really believe that Elfish had been lying to her about knowing someone who would help her with the funding, she could not put it entirely out of her mind.

Elfish accepted a cup of tea without grace, wishing that Shonen would offer her a proper drink.

"I'm up to line twenty-two and it's killing me. Let's do it."

Shonen fled the room and was gone for some time.

"I thought your vomiting was getting better," said Elfish impatiently as she returned.

"Do you really know someone who does funding?" blurted out Shonen, unable to approach the question as tactfully as she would have wished.

Elfish was untroubled by this. She looked straight into Shonen's eyes and told her with the utmost sincerity that she did indeed, making up on the spot a name and address to go with the tale. In this she was utterly convincing. Even the extreme stress and tension which Elfish was now undergoing did not diminish her ability to lie with total conviction.

Reassured, Shonen flung herself enthusiastically into helping Elfish and some progress was made. After immense effort Elfish could recite Mercutio's speech as far as line twenty-seven:

And sometimes comes she with a tithe-pig's tail

"What the hell does that mean?" demanded Elfish.

"How would I know?" said Shonen.

"Well, you're the actress. How is it the nation's greatest playwright couldn't write a line in plain English?"

Shonen said that it probably was plain English when it was written but Elfish was doubtful.

"I expect he made it obscure just so people would think he was clever. This Shakespeare is a total pain. It's way too complicated. Strong and direct, that's what a play should be," pronounced Elfish, who had never actually been to the theatre. "Direct and to the point like my guitar playing."

They struggled on for a while longer until Elfish grew enraged at the difficulty of it all and her bad temper sent Shonen hurrying nervously out of the room to be sick again. As there was nothing left inside Shonen to be sick with the spasms made her feel very ill. She had to bring the session to an end, much to Elfish's disgust.

"For God's sake, Shonen, get control of yourself. I'm the one who's doing all the work around here. It's me who's spending twenty-four hours a day trying to get a band together and learn this ridiculous fucking speech. Not to mention moving heaven and earth to find people to help your theatre group. All you have to do is eat, refrain from vomiting and teach me a few lines. Pull yourself together. I'll see you tomorrow."

Back home the cat was lying on the phone. Elfish booted it off, and figured she might as well make a phone call.

"Hey, Mo, how's things, it's Amnesia. Is Elfish still learning the speech?"

"I think so."

Elfish hooted with laughter, and painted a picture for Mo of the difficulties Elfish must be having, feeling that it would be best for him not to know that she was in fact making some progress.

"It was a brilliant agreement, Mo. Nothing could have made Elfish feel worse. When she tries to quote the speech on Saturday make sure there are plenty of people around. The poor bitch will die of embarrassment. I did hear from another friend that she's doing well with her band, though. That doesn't surprise me. You have to admit that Elfish is a determined woman. Unusually good guitarist as well. And an excellent stage diver."

In his house, Mo lay beside Amnesia, his hand on her breast, and smiled to himself.

"I thought you were a better stage diver, Amnesia."

"No, Elfish was better," said Elfish. "I remember the night she jumped clear off the speakers, walked over the hands of the audience till she reached the bar and bought a pint of lager. The same night she slept with Cody, I think."

There was a brief silence.

"Elfish slept with Cody?" said Mo, not sounding very pleased about it.

"Sure," said Elfish. "Didn't you know? They were always fond of each other. Cody used to recite Milton to her."

Mo took his hand off Amnesia's breast, and frowned.

"Oh well, see you soon," said Elfish, and rang off.

fifty-one

O! then, I see, Queen Mab hath been with you.
She is the fairies' midwife, and she comes
In shape no bigger than an agate-stone
On the fore-finger of an alderman,
Drawn with a team of little atomies
Athwart men's noses as they lie asleep:
Her waggon-spokes made of long spinners' legs;
The cover, of the wings of grasshoppers;
The traces, of the smallest spider's web;
The collars, of the moonshine's watery beams;

Elfish recited as she walked along Coldharbour Lane and imagined herself as Queen Mab, the deliverer of dreams, before being
distracted by a dope dealer outside a pub. Abandoning her recita-
tion temporarily, she began examining a cunning idea which had
occurred to her last night. It might work, and it appealed to her so
much that she was moved to twitch her lips, which she imagined
was a smile.

Police cars roared past, sirens blaring, a sight and sound so common as to raise no interest. Elfish screwed up her eyes against the sun

and made some mental calculations. Having discovered through the credulousness of Shonen, Casaubon and Aisha that people would believe anything if they were desperate enough for it to be true, she now planned to play cynically on both the politics and emotions of Marion, Chevon, Gail and Perlita and recruit them to her cause.

She found them sitting in the large downstairs room in a pall of gloom. This room was half white and half filthy grey, a sudden enthusiasm for painting having expired with the magazine. Unfriendly eyes regarded her as she entered.

Pitching her voice at an aggressive whine she started in on them immediately, mocking them for their defeatism.

"Still sitting around depressed because you couldn't raise any money or find a distributor? What a pathetic bunch you are. I've never known anyone give up so easily. If you really believed in your damned newspaper you'd work something out, you'd get the money somewhere and you'd take it round the shops on your bicycles or sell it on the streets or something. You just can't be bothered to make the effort. Like everyone else around here you would prefer just to give up. And you have the nerve to level criticisms against me for being antisocial? Who could be sociable towards a bunch of down-and-out fakes and failures like yourselves?"

Her flatmates, suffering this criticism from Elfish about something she had never shown the slightest interest in, were shocked and perplexed. Elfish ignored their protests and carried on.

"And when an opportunity to help yourselves does arise, what happens? You ignore it. When the one person who could be of use to you is on the verge of great things, what do you do? You abuse her. And why? Because you'd rather sit around being depressed, that's why. You enjoy it. It makes you feel good. You get pleasure from your misery. You're shallow. You're sick. You blame the President of

America and McDonald's hamburgers for your troubles in Brixton and then you don't have to do anything else except sit around whingeing about negative images on television. You've never tried for anything in your lives, you never will, you'll never have any effect on the world because you don't really want to."

Elfish spat on the floor, and stormed up to her room.

Well, that ought to do it, she mused cheerfully.

Pigeons scampered around the roof. It always surprised Elfish the amount of noise that pigeons' feet could make through a roof. She put on a Babes in Toyland album at immense volume to drown them out.

Human footsteps sounded on the stairs. Chevon's head appeared round Elfish's door.

"What opportunity for success?" she said, wincing at the noise and the humid, incense-laden air.

fifty-two

CARY AND LILAC were keen lovers but they did not have sex as often as observers of their public affection might have imagined, because much of the time they were too stoned. They could make love while powerfully under the influence of grass or ecstasy, their usual drugs, and even while tripping, but often the drugs made them more prone to lying on their mattress in a fond embrace without actually doing anything much.

On occasion, however, after taking ecstasy, they would find themselves projected into a strange and pleasantly elongated world wherein they had the energy and inclination to make love even after dancing for twelve hours, which they would do at raves. Then Lilac would slide his small body down over Cary's pale white thighs and lick her cunt for a long, long time. Cary would lie happily like this for an age before sliding herself over on top of Lilac and taking his cock in her mouth, and suck him in a very gentle manner. In this way they would spend the remaining hours of their wakefulness, passing into a kind of tantric and ecstatic state of pleasurable feeling before eventually drifting off to sleep, feeling that they were very much in love and everything in the world was good.

"Soon we'll have enough money for our holiday," whispered Cary, and this made the world seem especially fine.

Unfortunately for Cary she was mistaken in this, being unaware that their savings had dramatically shrunk due to Elfish's urgent need for a pair of sunglasses.

Sunglasses were a problem for Elfish. The pain that the sun caused her made it important for her to have some and the upcoming gig made it vital that they looked good. When she walked on stage with Queen Mab she did not intend to be wearing a bad pair of shades. Unfortunately, to her surprise, she had found that good sunglasses were expensive. There were many pairs on sale in Brixton, hanging in racks outside the bargain shops alongside baseball caps and unbranded washing-up liquid, but none of them were at all satisfactory. The only pair good enough were sitting in the window of a chemist and they were outrageously expensive.

Where could she get some money from immediately? Pacing her room in frustration, a picture suddenly formed in her mind of Cary and Lilac burying something in their garden. It struck her forcefully that it could well be money because any money they had would have to be hidden from Dennis's overwhelming desire to drink Special Brew all the time.

It was the work of only a few seconds to climb the garden wall, scrabble around in the dirt and remove the tin, thereby dashing her young neighbours' hopes of a quiet week away from the city.

Afterwards, posing with some enthusiasm in front of a shop window, Elfish was pleased. They were excellent sunglasses. And she was satisfied to have robbed Cary and Lilac, who continually tormented her, and had had the effrontery to involve themselves in a painting of Queen Mab.

fifty-three

ARAN HAD A strong temptation to program Elfish into his video game but was undecided as to whether she was about to bring off a spectacular triumph or plunge into disaster. He decided against it anyway. Elfish would not be pleased to find her own brother suspecting that she was not going to fulfil her dream. Aran was aware that Elfish, now with no real friends, had come to depend on him for support.

He stared at his computer terminal. It was becoming a little tedious simply sweeping the raft towards the edge of the world all the time. Aran programed in a new level where it disappeared down the middle of a whirlpool, landing in a gloomy underground world full of trolls and serpents.

Aran's game was actually even more tedious than he imagined because he had no real idea of how to make a game work well. Anyone other than himself would have seen it for the ridiculous thing that it was. Still, an author who has abandoned writing as a stupid endeavour has to do something.

Once underground the adventurers had the opportunity to find their way back to safety by following a silken thread laid out like the one that led Theseus safely from the maze after slaying the Minotaur. Following this, however, led immediately to a place where the path branched off into sixty tunnels, only one of which led to the way out.

Aran chuckled as his mythical and historical characters failed to find the way out.

"Looks like it's back to the ocean for you," he said, as they were forced by dragons down a deep well which brought them once more on to their raft and right up to the final waterfall of doom.

He was not entirely happy with this level. What if someone managed to pick the right way out? It was sixty to one but that was not a chance Aran was willing to take. He reworked it a little, placing a vast army of trolls at the end of the one correct tunnel to chase off anyone who made it that far.

Ben Jonson, Cleopatra, Pericles, Botticelli, Mick Ronson, Bomber Harris and Red Sonja, battered by their underground struggle with the trolls, sat grim-faced as the raft teetered on the brink of the void. Among them was another dark and mysterious figure who seemed to have appeared from nowhere; no one knew who she was and she did not speak.

fifty-four

IT WAS TIME for Elfish to rehearse. Aran walked down to the studio with his sister, helping her with her equipment. He noticed that Elfish's normally dour features were set into something that could almost have been a smile.

"Things are going well, I take it?"

"Line twenty-seven. And that's not all."

She pointed to her sunglasses. Aran admired them, telling her she was bound to look cool on stage.

Elfish had further reason to be satisfied. She informed Aran that in one magnificent stroke she had turned round the situation in her house. Instead of four harridans from hell waiting to pounce on her and toss her out into the street, Elfish now had four enthusiastic helpers willing her on to victory. The house, only yesterday a repository of gloom and despair, was, according to Elfish, now a hive of youthful and positive activity. It had taken her some effort to do this as her natural inclination was to distress her flatmates rather than cheer them up, but Elfish had deemed it necessary for her purposes.

The tale she told Aran was impressive indeed. It showed again the vast range of Elfish's imaginative powers in matters pertaining to her own advancement. In answer to Chevon's enquiry about what opportunity for success presented itself, Elfish had pointed out that even someone as dense and insular as Chevon had no doubt noticed that Elfish was getting her band together again. Were Chevon only to look at the matter properly she would see that this was good news for the magazine because the fund-raising possibilities of Elfish's band were limitless.

"If you and your friends were to get behind me in matters of promoting gigs and suchlike we would already have a solid base for making money. Not a great deal round here, I admit, but you probably only need a few hundred pounds to get the magazine off to a good start. We could easily raise that. But that would only be the beginning. Now this next thing is strictly confidential . . ."

Elfish then related, quite untruthfully but entirely convincingly, that for the past three months she had been secretly sleeping with Adam, Brixton's only rock star. His band was a phenomenon in that they were based in Brixton and were successful. They were so successful that they toured the world and released records that sold in millions.

This was true about the band, and Adam's walls were lined with gold records, but he never socialised in Brixton and neither Elfish nor anyone she knew had ever actually met him.

"And he has promised me that we can support him in some gigs. As he has a regular girlfriend who would not be particularly pleased to learn that I have been shagging him, I think I can count on his promise. Adam in fact is a very right-on musician. He is not above helping good causes and there is every reason to suppose that were I to ask him at an appropriate moment, for instance when I am giving him a blow-job, if his band would do a benefit for the magazine, he might well agree."

"And did this work?" asked Aran.

"It did indeed. The prospect of money won them over entirely. They are as venal as everybody else. They are now working for me on the definite understanding that prosperous benefit gigs will follow soon. What's more, Gail is going to borrow a bass guitar and play for me on Saturday so my band is complete. She is a lousy guitarist and will probably be even worse on bass but at least she'll be there. My guitar will cover up most of what she plays anyway. Also they will bring along their friends to the gig which is good because they have lots of friends and I get a split of the door.

"I had further arguments in reserve, such as pointing out that as a woman I should be supported in my struggle with Mo, especially as I may end up in a position in which he can demand anything he desires, but by that time I had won my case anyway. All in all a complete triumph, I'm sure you'll agree."

Elfish frowned slightly though, at the very thought of losing to Mo. Aran carried her guitar into the rehearsal rooms under the arches.

"You haven't actually ever met Adam the rock star, have you?"

Elfish shook her head.

"If your band got going, would you play benefits for the magazine?"

"You must be joking," said Elfish. "Fuck benefits. I wouldn't sully the name of Queen Mab. This is rock and roll."

fifty-five

AFTER LEAVING ELFISH to her rehearsal Aran was immediately depressed. He ignored the beggar who hung around outside the studio, optimistic after receiving money from May, and wandered off aimlessly.

He wondered who he could go to and tell about his unhappiness. No one sprang to mind. Each of his few friends was a long way past their tolerance limit as regards Aran's continual depression.

His day of discomfort at the heat and aimless unhappiness did contain one small success when he found card number three in his second packet of cigarettes.

"Right!" said Aran. "Number three. No doubt sent to Brixton due to a packaging error at the factory."

Now he had only one card left to collect. The five pounds was almost his.

After this, however, he had nothing at all to do. Nothing interested him. A cluster of unwanted people who sat regularly on a bench on a wide corner asked him for cigarettes but Aran ignored them. His generosity, what there was of it, had disappeared with his girlfriend.

When a few hours of aimless wandering had brought him

nowhere he found himself back at the rehearsal studio. The band might be taking a break.

In this he was lucky. As he arrived Elfish was forcing coins into the coffee machine and hitting it to hurry the process along.

"What are you doing back here?" she asked, and Aran confessed that he had nothing better to do.

"Then why not go and keep Shonen happy?"

"What? Why?"

"Because I've been worried about her ever since I heard she slept with Mo. Any woman Mo has slept with becomes a prime suspect in my eyes, and needs careful watching."

"What if she doesn't want to be carefully watched?"

"She will. Shonen loves attention. All neurotics love attention. As long as you are prepared to listen to their problems, they're happy. Just politely ignore it when she leaves the room to vomit. Stay with her as long as you can, I don't want Mo getting back to her. I don't care what she learns after the gig is over but until then she has to stay on my side. So go and keep her happy." Elfish glanced at Aran's miserable face. "Well, perhaps that's asking too much. But keep her occupied. Be sympathetic about her bad childhood. Help her with her sponsorship forms. Talk about Shakespeare. Tell her stories. Fuck her."

"I can't."

"Why not? You're still fairly attractive and Shonen will probably sleep with anyone who's prepared to listen to her problems for long enough. I would do it myself because you know I always like to fuck Mo's lovers to annoy him but I haven't got time. Also, I must admit I find Shonen fairly disgusting these days. Listening to her neuroses for a few hours would drive me completely mad. But you'll be good at it. You like talking about personal problems. I'm sure if you can make it through to about four in the morning without falling asleep or displaying too much obvious boredom you'll probably just end up naturally in bed. Go and see Shonen and make yourself useful. Remember, I still need her because I'm stuck on the speech."

Leaving the studio, Aran remembered to his frustration that he had forgotten to tell Elfish about finding card number three. Perhaps he should go back.

He decided against it. Elfish probably wasn't as interested in his cards as she pretended to be. It struck him that he should have asked his sister how the rehearsal was going. Aran sighed. He could not do anything right these days. What was it about your girlfriend leaving you that made everything so bad?

He shook his head, and tried to walk, but each step felt difficult and he wondered if he should just throw himself under a car and get it over with. A truck would be better. He glanced around to see if there was anything suitable coming along the road. Then he realised that he couldn't throw himself under a truck just now as he was meant to be doing something for Elfish.

A strange and unrecognisable emotion crept into his soul. This unrecognisable emotion was something like a sense of purpose, although it was so long since Aran had had any sense of purpose he would have been unable even to put a name to it.

Elfish's unquenchable drive, which was even now pulling Shonen and the others along in its wake, was also getting to Aran.

Not looking where he was going, he bumped into Cary and Lilac. He cursed himself for his carelessness. Usually Aran kept a close lookout for the hated couple and would take long diversions to avoid having to deal with their cheerfulness.

To his amazement they were not cheerful. They were sad-faced and seemed to have been crying. They stood looking very small and hopeless among the busy crowds outside the tube station.

"Someone stole our money," they said.

The loss had been devastating to them. Their dreams of a holiday in the country had crumbled into nothing. Their optimistic spirits were crushed. It seemed too hard to start again. They would not now have a holiday. They assumed that Dennis had stolen their money to buy drink. Aran left them in the street, wandering around in purposeless depression.

Aran, who had not asked Elfish how she had paid for her expensive sunglasses, but knew her very well, had a better idea of where the money had gone. He marvelled at his sister's single-mindedness and capacity for direct action. What a woman. In one powerful move she had got herself an excellent item of apparel and delivered a much-needed lesson to Cary and Lilac. It was high time they discovered that life was not all dancing and putting daisies in each other's hair. He nodded in approval as he made his way down to Shonen's.

Back in the studio the rehearsal was going well and everyone's life felt better as the music rolled out, although Elfish's filthy appearance and manic behaviour was a little unsettling to the others. Also unsettling was her new habit of quoting Shakespeare at inappropriate moments. She now did this fairly often, apparently without realising what she was doing.

fifty-six

ELFISH'S PREDICTION CAME true. After listening to Shonen talk about her bulimia, her various other neuroses and their associated problems for five and a half hours, Aran did end up in bed with her. Unfortunately they had some difficulty in having sex. This was due to problems with condoms; that is, Aran found it difficult to put one on. With his stress, depression, increased drinking and huge cigarette consumption, Aran was no longer the potent young man he once had been, and he had found it increasingly difficult to get strong erections in recent sexual encounters. This made the condom a particular problem because the one thing you must have to use a condom is a firm erection. It was, as Aran found to his cost, no use simply trying to stuff a half-erect penis into one and hoping things would get better.

It had started off reasonably enough with Shonen, and he certainly found her thin body very attractive. When she gripped his penis it went hard quickly, or fairly quickly, but the instant he stretched over to remove the condom from its packet things went badly wrong. Reaching down eagerly to slide it on he found to his distress that his cock was no longer hard enough. Seeing his erection disappearing he tried to rush things but this only made matters worse.

"Oh dear," said Shonen.

"Yes," said Aran, and dived quickly to lick Shonen's vagina, partly to cover his embarrassment and partly to keep her from losing interest. Shonen squirmed on top of him to suck his cock and to Aran's relief it again went hard.

Now is the moment, he thought, and tore himself free to have another go with the prophylactic. His fingers fumbled nervously with the packet as he tried to rip it open, feeling instinctively that this was a race against time. The packet split apart but in Aran's eagerness he pushed his fingernail straight through the rubber.

"Well, that's not much fucking good," he snarled. "I thought these things were all electronically tested."

Shonen waited patiently as he reached for his third condom of the night. He opened this one more carefully and tried rolling it on but he was too late. His erection was fading sadly away, and a general numbness told him that it would be some time in returning.

"Well," said Shonen. "They are certainly an efficient method of contraception. There seems very little chance of me getting pregnant. What exactly is the problem?"

"Nothing at all," replied Aran. "Well, not much. I'm just not very good with condoms. They make my erections disappear."

Shonen seemed interested in this.

"Why?"

"I don't know."

"Have you seen a doctor?"

"I do not need to see a doctor," replied Aran defensively. "I just have a problem with condoms, that's all."

"Perhaps we should try again," suggested Shonen, always willing to help a lover in distress. "I'll grab your cock, make it go hard and then whip on a condom before it knows what's happening."

Aran's spirits revived. This seemed worth a try at least.

They got back to lovemaking and Aran tried to put the whole business out of his mind, running his hands over Shonen's body and kissing her with rather more enthusiasm than he normally managed in bed, trying to make up for his failure. Shonen meanwhile manipulated his penis in a fairly determined manner, having already opened a fourth condom, which now lay in readiness.

Judging the moment to be right, Shonen made her move, and fairly flew for the contraceptive. In a blur of movement she had it up and over Aran's penis before he had time to think.

"Success!" they cried together, and Shonen lay back, dragging Aran on top of her.

Aran's anti-condom complex had now become too powerful, however, and in the few seconds it took him to guide his penis between Shonen's legs it had again rebelled and was sinking back down into oblivion. Inside the condom, this made a distressing sight.

"I am a great fan of oral sex," said Aran. "Better than intercourse, probably," but he thought some bitter thoughts about all the huge erections he had woken up alone with in the morning, any of which would have served him well tonight.

fifty-seven

CARY AND LILAC tried to raise a little money by selling some cassettes in John Mackie's secondhand music shop. The sum they would earn by this would be very little indeed.

John Mackie looked at the cassettes without enthusiasm. While examining them he handed Cary a leaflet advertising Elfish's gig which was now just two days away.

"Be sure and go to this," he told them. "They are an excellent band. You'll get in one pound cheaper with this flier."

It did not strike Cary and Lilac that this was an odd person to be exhibiting such enthusiasm for Elfish because they were really too vague about the world to notice any of its oddities, but many people might have wondered why this elderly and uncommunicative man was suddenly showing such interest in the affair.

Caught up in Elfish's enthusiasm, John Mackie was now firmly committed to her success. He had given her equipment on credit and promised to hand out leaflets to all his customers. As he was now aware of Elfish's need to learn the speech, he was no longer distressed by her habit of mumbling blank verse while checking out a delay unit or a speaker cabinet. He encouraged her in her endeavours and told her that she was making good progress.

Elfish reminded him increasingly of his sister. Because of this John Mackie found that he could now imagine his sister as a real person rather than an idealised image. He remembered that she had been kind to him, and that she too had been musical. But she had not been perfect, she could be argumentative when it suited her. Now that he thought about it, his sister had never been too keen on washing, either. Perhaps if she had been born now she might have worn motorbike boots like Elfish. She might even have pierced her nose with a ring and a stud. This thought actually made him smile.

He felt much better about his sister now. When he lit candles for her soul at St. Mark's Church he would remember her fondly and wish her well instead of shaking his head grimly and feeling only pain.

"We will definitely go to the gig if we can raise the money," Cary and Lilac told him. "We are friends of Elfish."

The shop-owner was impressed by anyone being friends with Elfish and kept them talking for a while. He paid them rather more for their old cassettes than they were worth. So impressed was he that he asked if either of them would like the job he was advertising as Saturday Assistant.

Cary and Lilac were a little taken aback to be offered a proper job, even for one day a week. It would be an unusual departure into the real world for them. They agreed, provided they could share the work.

John Mackie was pleased. He was happy to have friends of Elfish's working for him. Cary and Lilac were pleased. They were happy to have the opportunity to earn a little money. They could again start saving for their holiday.

fifty-eight

ARAN WAS NOT pleased to be woken by Elfish at ten o'clock in the morning.

"Beer," she said. "Quickly."

Aran followed her through to the fridge where she was already ripping the top off a bottle with the buckle on her jacket.

"I take it Mo has sent you another Queen Mab poem?"

Elfish tore a sheet of paper from her pocket and brandished it at Aran. He was impressed to see that it was a photocopied picture of Queen Mab as depicted by Blake, the famous English poet and artist. He read the caption underneath and saw that it was from Blake's illustrations for Milton's "L'Allegro." As "L'Allegro" was the poem from which Elfish had last sent a verse to Mo this was certainly an impressive comeback.

"I sent him a poem by Milton and now he's found a picture of the same poem by Blake and sent it back," wailed Elfish. "It's no good, I can't win. Obviously Cody is undefeatable when it comes to obscure Queen Mab references."

"He certainly is not," said Aran, greatly offended. "I will find you another long-forgotten Queen Mab poem in no time. Depend on it. I refuse to let Cody or anyone else know more about English

Literature than me. So calm yourself, Elfish, and let an expert take over."

Elfish stared at him in astonishment. This was the most positive statement she could ever remember Aran making.

They drank beer for breakfast and listened to Carter's "Under the Thumb and Over the Moon." The alcohol calmed Elfish down a little and in the cool gloom of Aran's flat she relaxed slightly.

"So you slept with Shonen," she said. "I trust she is now firmly back on my side?"

Aran was non-committal about this although he claimed to have done his best.

"How is the speech going?"

Elfish shuddered. Her relaxation vanished and on her next attempt at the bottle, beer dribbled down her chin, clearing away a little dirt. The gig was tomorrow. She was too busy to think straight, she had not slept or eaten and was keeping going with amphetamines. She took another beer and buried her head in Shonen's coloured copy of Mercutio's speech and refused to discuss it further.

Aran studied her as she read. He smiled, almost. Considering Elfish's recent activities, he was lost in admiration. Aisha, only last week a tangle of jagged nerves, panic attacks and phobias, all competing for space with her catastrophic depression over her ex-boyfriend Mory, was now transformed. Elfish's assertion that Mory was coming back and her action in giving Aisha a useful task to perform had worked something that seemed like a miracle. Now Aisha spent her days busily painting a huge black sheet to hang behind the band. According to Casaubon, who had been helping her, she showed few signs of nerves and her agoraphobia had receded to the point where she could now go round to the local shop by herself.

Casaubon himself had suffered a similar transformation and the prospect of seeing his ex-girlfriend Marcia at the gig and sorting out their relationship had breathed fresh life into him. His depression was gone, he was happy painting with Aisha and in between times he was playing his drum kit as never before.

The same could be said for May. Anyone who had known her in the past few months would have described her as an excellent candidate for suicide, but Elfish's offer of a secure place to live seemed to have got to the very root of her problems. She was now both playing the guitar and sorting out her life. She had been down to the unemployment office and signed on, something she had been incapable of before, and promised her friends that after the gig she would find some sort of work to repay her debts. Meanwhile, she practised her guitar every day. Her playing was by all accounts demonic. Even the bored and music-weary attendant at the rehearsal studio had paused, looked up from his newspaper, and nodded appreciatively to himself as the shrieking and demented sound of May and Elfish playing guitar together floated out through the walls of the imperfectly soundproofed practice room.

Shonen had filled in every one of her funding forms and made a start on combing through her large directory of organisations who might give them some sponsorship. Her renewed enthusiasm had apparently brought her ossified theatre group back to life. In various parts of South London the young men and women of the group were deciding that no, they would not try and get a part in an Andrew Lloyd Webber musical, but stick to the task they believed in. They were now trying harder than ever to impersonate buildings, crows, aeroplanes and DNA molecules. (Think of the immense spirit contained within a DNA molecule!) Already discussions about a new production were under way. Shonen's bulimia was too deep-seated to be shifted by an improvement of her mood but she was bingeing

and vomiting far less. When Aisha had phoned her at Elfish's suggestion to share their troubles, Shonen had taken seriously for the first
time ever a suggestion that she should seek some sort of help.

Equally as remarkable was the transformation Elfish had wrought
on her own household. Just two days before, the only communication between Elfish and her flatmates had been in the form of
mutual abuse. Elfish had been banished to her room, a pariah, hated
by all. Meanwhile, the four young women sat downstairs, unhap-
pily pondering the ruins of their dream of starting a magazine. Now
they were busy getting articles together, planning layouts and phoning up printers for quotes, confident that it would happen one day,
and possibly soon. Gail was actually playing bass for Elfish and in
between magazine work the women were tirelessly publicising the
gig. They were telling all their friends, and there were many of them,
to come along, making sure they brought fliers for Elfish's band. The
point of this was that not only was admission cheaper with a leaflet
but the more of them that were handed in the larger Elfish's split of
the takings would be.

So the house was suddenly a place of cheerful activity, and if Elfish
was no more friendly herself than before, no one minded. They put
it down to the quite understandable stress of getting a band ready
for a gig at such short notice, and excused her.

When Aran heard later that day that Cary and Lilac had gained
employment in a music shop entirely because they knew Elfish it
seemed to him that his sister must now be spreading a benevolent
magic over the very ground on which she walked.

Musing on all these changes Aran realised that he himself had not
been unaffected. Whereas before he had sat for weeks on end in his
darkened room, too depressed to move, now he was out and about
picking up things for Elfish, taking messages, checking equipment,

and so on. On the night of the gig he was to act as roadie and help set up the equipment. He was looking forward to this. It was a long time since he had looked forward to anything. And just a few moments ago he had positively leapt at the challenge of finding a new poem for his sister, something he would have strenuously avoided doing only a few days before.

He gazed at Elfish and marvelled. Because of her a host of shattered and defeated people seemed to have come back to life. That Elfish, enemy of humanity, should be responsible for all this was almost beyond belief. The thought crossed his mind that perhaps his sister might actually be some sort of latter-day saint. With her filthy skin, rancid hair, ragged clothes and wild eyes, she was even beginning to look the part.

He remembered, though, that everything Elfish was doing was entirely towards her own ends, each action pushing her along till she could fulfil her passionate desire to claim the name of Queen Mab for her own. And each action had started off with a lie, possibly a serious and damaging lie, the effects of which would surely soon make themselves felt in the most painful way possible. Aran frowned. As far as he could see, Elfish was doomed. He could only hope that her doom did not arrive until after the gig.

fifty-nine

MO WAS PLANNING a more comprehensive doom for Elfish than Aran could possibly imagine. Through his many friends in Brixton he was aware of all the varied promises that Elfish had made to people and he knew them all to be untrue. He intended to use this knowledge to crush Elfish.

He now realised that he might have acted too hastily in trying to turn Shonen against Elfish. Elfish had had time to convince Shonen of her sincerity and she was a supremely convincing liar. Mo would not make the same mistake again.

All in all, Mo was confident of defeating his enemy and his life felt good, especially with Amnesia around. As a couple they got on very well. The only small blemish on his existence was the occasional presence of Cary and Lilac in his flat. Mo was no more enthusiastic about them than anyone else. Each time they waltzed in holding hands and looking lovingly at each other he wished mournfully that Cody could have picked someone else to model for him.

Elfish was still beset with problems, the main one being the speech. She just could not learn under such pressure. Line twenty-seven was her absolute limit and even that was shaky. Tonight she was visiting Shonen yet again and if she failed once more she would have no other opportunity. Not surprisingly, although she had successfully contrived to get everyone she needed working for her, her mood did not lighten and her tension did not lift. Her lips became tighter, her eyes narrower, and her distress at the heat more acute.

To protect her eyes from the sun Elfish wore her new and impenetrable sunglasses. Over these her beaded fringes formed a second line of defence. The beads would chatter lightly on the lenses as she turned her head this way and that, as she was now prone to do in her nervousness. On her head she wore a black baseball cap with the peak angled sharply down so that her face was barely visible. With the fringes, sunglasses and angled hat, and her head tilted well forward when she walked, it was hard to see how she could even put one foot in front of the other without crashing into something.

When she was forced to emerge from these layers of protection, as for instance when reading the speech, she blinked and strained as if in pain, even in the gloom of Aran's flat.

"I can't remember it," she said flatly.

"Tonight at Shonen's you'll succeed," Aran told her. Unfortunately his voice was patently insincere. Elfish scowled at him.

"Damn right I will."

sixty

ELFISH SUFFERED TOTAL failure at Shonen's. Not one line of Mercutio's speech would lodge in her mind although after so many repetitions Shonen now knew the speech herself. The actress had picked it up easily, without even trying.

Shonen, by now a very enthusiastic supporter of Elfish's efforts, encouraged, cajoled, bullied and pleaded with Elfish to remember her lines but Elfish just could not do it. The knowledge of Mo's animosity towards her, the strain of getting her band together, the continual appearance of poems and fragments of writing about Queen Mab and the constant gossiping and questioning of her acquaintances and enemies had affected her to too great an extent.

"I'm defeated," said Elfish.

"You are never defeated," said Shonen.

"This time I am. See you at the gig."

Elfish's face was set in a grim frown. She picked up the speech and left. The night was humid and Elfish sweated inside her leather jacket as she walked through Shonen's estate. The moon shone down but it did not bring her comfort. Nor did the two men who crossed the road to follow her, forcing Elfish to accelerate, hurrying along till she reached the relative security of the main street. Elfish reflected grimly that if she lived in some country where guns were freely available she would have no qualms about shooting anyone who followed her along a dark street.

Around one in the morning she was sitting alone with a beer in a bar full of late drinkers. She looked tired, dirty and defeated. She was thinking for the first time ever that she really was going to fail. This had not occurred to her before. When she had claimed previously that it was all too difficult she had not actually believed it. Now she did.

Melancholy overwhelmed her. She could feel her dreams slowly seeping their way out of her body and disappearing towards the moon.

Elfish sipped her beer and thought about her band, and thought about Mo. They used to have good times together, playing pool in the pub, drinking, playing guitar, going to gigs. They had good times in bed as well. Rather unwillingly she found herself thinking of a morning when she had woken up before him. She had risen from bed and dressed and was about to leave when she noticed that Mo, still asleep, was looking particularly attractive. So she leant over to kiss him and he opened his eyes and grinned at her, at which Elfish simply threw back the bedclothes, pulled down her leggings, sat on top of him and fucked him. Mo, still bleary-eyed, did little except lie there smiling. Elfish, aroused by being fully dressed in her heavy leather jacket and motorbike boots, on top of Mo who was naked, warm and unusually passive, came quickly and departed. Mo went back to sleep. Elfish remembered it fondly. Or bitterly, she was not sure which. At least she could remember it which was more than could be said for some of her more recent sexual encounters.

A young man sat down beside her, introducing himself as Joseph. Elfish rudely told him to disappear. He offered her a beer. Elfish accepted it and told him she still wanted him to disappear.

"I recognise you," he said. "You used to know Mo. I know Mo. Only last week I was in bed with him."

Elfish looked up in wonderment. She could barely imagine Mo being in bed with a man.

"That's difficult to believe."

The young man told her various personal details about Mo and it seemed that he had indeed been in bed with Mo.

Elfish looked at Joseph in a more interested manner. He seemed to have money to spare and bought more beer for them both. Elfish, close to defeat and in need of comfort, accepted one drink after another. She sucked down the alcohol as quickly as it was provided and was soon drunk. It did cross her mind that this was her very last chance to go home and attempt to learn the speech but she did not have the willpower to try again.

Joseph asked if he could accompany her home. Elfish examined him. He was not unattractive, with long messy hair like Mo's and a denim jacket that was rotting with age.

Elfish generally liked fucking Mo's lovers. They walked back to her house together, with Elfish leaning drunkenly on his shoulder for support. Joseph produced a flat half bottle of whisky from his inside pocket and Elfish was soon totally intoxicated. She had to be helped up the stairs to her bedroom. She was far too drunk actually to do anything with Joseph. Trying to undress was a seemingly impossible series of actions involving her arms getting stuck in the ripped lining of her jacket and her leggings becoming tangled somewhere between her thighs and her motorbike boots. This did not mean she was not enjoying the experience. Joseph was reasonably attractive and having sex with him would probably take her mind off her imminent defeat.

She was, however, unable to do anything demonstrative like put her arms around Joseph, or kiss him, or keep her eyes open. She fell asleep several times while taking her clothes off, waking each time to a room that was spinning round her head. Elfish was too drunk to carry it through. Just at the point of intercourse she vomited in a powerful stream that splashed over Joseph's face and neck. Joseph, proving himself to be far less hardy than Aba had been, was utterly appalled, and angrily rose from the bed.

"You're disgusting," he said, wiping his face with one of Elfish's T-shirts, a poor choice as far as cleanliness was concerned. He threw on his clothes. At the door he turned and looked contemptuously at the semi-conscious Elfish.

"I never slept with Mo. But Mo told me you'd fuck me if I said I had. He asked me to sleep with you tonight to prevent you getting on with your speech. I guess I've succeeded in that anyway, though I wouldn't even have tried if I'd known how filthy your body was."

Joseph walked out of the room. Elfish lay still for a few moments. Using all her reserves of willpower she opened her eyes. She dragged herself on to her hands and knees and crawled downstairs. In the toilet she was sick again. Drink, tension and lack of sleep had severely weakened her constitution and she struggled to control her trembling limbs. She splashed water on to her face and tried to drive away her nausea by sheer willpower.

"Very clever, Mo," muttered Elfish with venom. "Enough to defeat a lesser woman. Fortunately I am not a lesser woman."

Furious and appalled at the dark treachery of his plotting she began to haul herself back up the stairs. Inside her small body her dreams and ambitions were welling up with renewed vigour.

sixty-one

THE RAFT CAME thundering out of the underground cavern and plunged over the huge roaring waterfall at the edge of the world. This was surely the end. Even Red Sonja, bravest of Barbarian warriors, screamed in fear. The ocean, slipping off the edge of the planet, cast a vast, violent spray of water far out into space. Each of the doomed souls clung on in terror as the huge volume of cascading water carried them down into the limitless void.

This is the end, thought Mick Ronson, miserably, his guitar now waterlogged and unplayable. And I still think I should have been more successful.

This is the end, thought Cleopatra, her fine Egyptian clothes and make-up ragged and smeared. And I should not have lost my kingdom.

This is the end, thought Bomber Harris. But I refuse to admit I was wrong to destroy an enemy city in wartime.

This is the end, thought Pericles, and was angry again with the Athenians who had exiled him.

This is the end, thought Ben Jonson, and prepared to meet his death in a very bad humour.

"Look!"

Botticelli, who would never paint again, was pointing through the thundering waters at a shadowy figure who flew alongside. As the figure approached they recognised her as the mysterious black-clad woman who had shared the last part of their journey.

Pericles and Red Sonja wearily unsheathed their swords, readying themselves to fight off a fresh attack.

"Prepare to repel boarders," howled Cleopatra.

"Who are you?" demanded Pericles.

"I am Queen Mab," said the stranger. "I have come to rescue you."

sixty-two

O! then, I see, Queen Mab hath been with you.
She is the fairies' midwife, and she comes
In shape no bigger than an agate-stone
On the fore-finger of an alderman,
Drawn with a team of little atomies
Athwart men's noses as they lie asleep:
Her waggon-spokes made of long spinners' legs;
The cover, of the wings of grasshoppers;
The traces, of the smallest spider's web;
The collars, of the moonshine's watery beams;
Her whip, of cricket's bone; the lash, of film;
Her waggoner, a small grey-coated gnat,
Not half so big as a round little worm
Prick'd from the lazy finger of a maid;
Her chariot is an empty hazel-nut,
Made by the joiner squirrel or old grub,
Time out o' mind the fairies' coach-makers.
And in this state she gallops night by night
Through lovers' brains, and then they dream of love;
O'er courtiers' knees, that dream on curtsies straight;

O'er lawyers' fingers, who straight dream on fees;
O'er ladies' lips, who straight on kisses dream;
Which oft the angry Mab with blisters plagues,
Because their breaths with sweetmeats tainted are.
Sometimes she gallops o'er a courtier's nose,
And then he dreams of smelling out a suit;
And sometimes comes she with a tithe-pig's tail,
Tickling a parson's nose as a' lies asleep,
Then dreams he of another benefice;
Sometime she driveth o'er a soldier's neck,
And then dreams he of cutting foreign throats,
Of breaches, ambuscadoes, Spanish blades,
Of healths five fathoms deep; and then anon
Drums in his ear, at which he starts and wakes;
And, being thus frighted, swears a prayer or two,
And sleeps again. This is that very Mab
That plats the manes of horses in the night:
And bakes the elf-locks in foul sluttish hairs,
Which once untangled much misfortune bodes;
This is the hag, when maids be on their backs,
That presses them and learns them first to bear,
Making them women of good carriage:
This is she.

Elfish had learned the speech. She dropped the book and fell asleep on the floor.

sixty-three

ON THE MORNING of the gig Aran got up early for the first time in four years. After some serious research he was now heavily armed with Queen Mab poems. He planned to put one through Mo's door and keep the rest in reserve for emergencies.

> Queen Mab and her light maydes the while,
> Amongst themselves doe closely smile,
> To see the King caught with this wile,
> With one another jesting:
> And to the Fayrie Court they went,
> With mickle joy and merriment,
> Which thing was done with good intent,
> And thus I left them feasting.
>
> —DRAYTON

That'll show him, thought Aran, and hurried home to sleep off the effects of his strenuous early morning.

He was woken by Elfish some time in the late afternoon. It was time to get ready for the gig. She had borrowed a van and Casaubon was driving round picking everyone up.

Elfish was pleased when Aran told her about the poem.

"Reports have reached me that Mo and Cody are looking uneasy, which is good. They know I've got them on the run."

Later Aran related some more news at which his sister professed to be amazed.

"I can't believe it. You ended your video game with an easy level where Queen Mab comes and rescues everyone? So anyone playing it can actually win?"

"That's right."

"Why?"

Aran explained that he had suffered a surprise attack of positive thinking.

"Because of you, I suppose, Elfish. Since you've been on this Queen Mab mania I haven't felt so bad about things. It seems difficult to be completely depressed when you're going around getting things done all the time."

Aran sounded just a little reproachful at this, as he had set his mind quite firmly on being completely depressed. Elfish had dragged him out of it, though, and he was now sitting beside her in the borrowed van with the rest of the musicians travelling the short distance to the gig.

Elfish was exhausted but the mood in the van was lighthearted. The band took Elfish's learning the speech as an excellent omen and in the few spare moments they had had today they had informed as many people as they could, encouraging them to come along and witness Elfish's triumph. As Mo had been doing the same for precisely the opposite reasons, tonight's event had every prospect of being much busier than would normally be expected for an unknown pair of bands playing in a pub in Brixton.

Aisha sat beside Casaubon in the front with the black sheet on which she had painted the backdrop resting on her knees. It was a beautiful backdrop, a painting of Queen Mab in her regal fairy glory travelling down from the moon to bring dreams to the earth. Around her were rainbow-hued fairy attendants, golden cosmic dust and silver shooting stars.

The lingering remnants of Aisha's agoraphobia made her slightly uncomfortable to be this far away from home but she had insisted on coming because she believed that Mory would be there. As well as this she said that it was important to her to hang the backdrop personally and see Elfish play in front of it.

Elfish herself was slightly cleaner, at least around the parts that were visible. Marion had produced a damp cloth before she left and wiped her face and hands.

"And you can't get much more friendly than that," said Shonen, who was with them in the van as an encouragement to Elfish. "Are you sure you remember every line?"

Elfish nodded confidently.

"She was driven by extreme fury beyond the effects of tension into a state of transcendental self-belief," said Aran.

"What?"

"I was so annoyed I learned the speech," said Elfish.

"Right."

Elfish had been yawning during the journey but as the van pulled up outside the venue she pushed aside the remnants of her stress and exhaustion and leapt out, guitar in hand. She strode inside as rock star and conquering hero.

Although the venue was only the side room of a bar, it was a place where regular gigs were held which meant that they had their own PA. Mo's band had not yet arrived so Elfish and her companions immediately started to set up their equipment for a soundcheck. This had to be done quickly because when the main band did arrive they would take precedence and the support act would quite possibly be granted no more time at all to check things out before going on stage.

"Two fingers," said Elfish as Aran laid a microphone over the small speaker cabinet she would be playing through. This microphone picked up the sound and took it via the mixing desk to the larger amplifiers and speakers of the sound system. She showed him how to measure the gap between the microphone and the speaker by placing two fingers between them. In this way she would know how to position it exactly correctly before they played because all the positioning of mikes they made just now would of course be changed when Mo sound-checked and there would be no opportunity to test the volume levels and balance again.

By the time Mo and his companions arrived Elfish had got things more or less how she wanted them, although this had caused a fair amount of animosity between herself and the woman who was doing the sound. Elfish naturally took it as a personal insult if her guitar did not sound just right.

She laid her instrument down in its case next to May's on a small shelf beside the stage. There was no dressing room.

"Where will we tune up?" asked May. Elfish shrugged. Tuning up carefully together before going on stage had never been one of her strongest concerns.

The room was already filling up. Unusually, people were arriving early and this was no doubt due to the now well publicised confrontation that was to take place.

Mo and Elfish made no contact and their respective entourages hung around on opposite sides of the bar avoiding each other. Elfish had been expecting some adverse reaction when Aisha and Aran pinned up the Queen Mab backdrop but there was none.

"Perhaps he knows he's beaten already," said Elfish.

"Look at all these people," said Shonen, anxiously drinking a pint. "It makes me nervous."

"Everything makes you nervous."

"Mory isn't here yet," said Aisha, looking round.

"He will be," said Elfish, and walked away before anyone else bothered her with their problems. She went to stand alone outside the door to prepare herself. This turned out to be a bad move because as she stood there Joseph arrived. He grinned at her. Elfish glared furiously back at him but swallowed the abuse she was about to deliver because she knew it was vital that she remain calm. Any undue stress might drive the speech out of her head. Slightly shaken, she hurried back for another pint and a word with Shonen.

Fortunately, she found that seeing Joseph had not banished her lines from her memory, but it had been close.

"Stay calm," whispered Shonen, which brought a retort from Elfish so stinging that Shonen was obliged to hurry away to the toilet and be sick. Aran was relieved to see that his sister's need for help had not actually made her decide to be unnecessarily pleasant to anyone.

sixty-four

THE ROOM WAS now full. People queued eight deep at the bar. Some waited patiently while others brandished money and shouted their orders to the harassed-looking bar staff. Across from here was the stage, a fairly high stage for a small room, and the rough concrete in front of this was the only unoccupied area in the whole venue. As there was no dressing room, both bands' equipment was piled up beside the stage while the bands themselves struggled at the bar along with everyone else.

Tula and Lizzy, the last of Elfish's former friends to desert her, were in the audience, but they did not speak to Elfish or wish her well.

At the bar Aran found himself next to Cody.

"Well, I guess we won when it came to the Queen Mab poems," said Aran, smugly.

"Nonsense," retorted Cody. "A few well-known poems count for nothing."

"What do you mean 'well-known?'" demanded Aran. "Drayton's 'Nimphidia' is not a well-known poem."

"It is to me. Much better known than Jonson's 'Entertainment.' Now that's what I call an obscure work."

"Preposterous," snorted Aran. "I read it when I was in primary school. And *The Alchemist.* Queen Mab's in that as well."

"So? Everyone knows that. You didn't know Blake painted a picture of Milton's 'L'Allegro,' did you?"

"Of course I did. I have a copy hanging on my wall."

"How about this?" demanded Cody. "'A dwarf to thrust aside, a wicked mage to stab, and, Lo ye, I had kissed Queen Mab.'"

"Browning's 'Easter Day,'" said Aran. "Not one of my favourites, unlike 'Oh fairy, come attend our royal grace, Let's go and share our fruit with our Queen Mab.' No doubt you are unfamiliar with that?"

"Randolph's 'Amyntas,'" replied Cody immediately, to Aran's great annoyance, and suddenly the air was full of verse as the pair tried to prove which one of them was the most knowledgeable. Lines from Porlis's "Parnassus," Brown's "Britannia's Pastorals" and the anonymous "History of Jacob and Esau" rent the air with increasing vehemence.

"I refuse to believe you have actually read 'Brittania's Pastorals,'" shouted Aran, and they began to jostle each other.

The affair was brought to an abrupt end by the arrival of Mo who pulled Cody away. He gave him a withering look.

"Stop this stupidity," he ordered.

Elfish"s time had arrived.

"Well?" said Mo.

"Well, what?"

"Are you going to back out of it?"

"No," said Elfish. "I'm not. And you are still stupid."

Elfish began elbowing her way towards the front, followed by her band. It was time for the fulfilment of her dream.

No one else present had Elfish's tenacity in pursuing their dreams but that did not mean they had none of their own. Following Elfish closely, cheap guitar in hand, was May, who dreamed of having no more nightmares about her time in prison in Ireland and a secure place to live in London. Behind May was Casaubon the drummer who dreamed of his girlfriend moving back in with him and forgiving him for his terrible behaviour. Behind Casaubon was Gail with her borrowed bass guitar. She dreamed of her magazine being successful, or even existing, and she carried along with her the dreams of Marion, Chevon and Perlita, who were standing in the crowd, wishing her well.

At the front of the audience stood Aisha, studying with pleasure the backdrop she had painted and hung, and dreaming of her agoraphobia disappearing and Mory reappearing. She glanced anxiously around her, wondering why he had not shown up yet. Beside her was Shonen, pointing out proudly to the rest of her theatre group the small figure of Elfish, who was going to rescue them, and her companions said what a striking and impressive figure Elfish was, and commented that Shonen herself seemed much healthier these days.

Next to them was Aran, dreaming of selling his video game to a large company, and collecting all twenty cigarette cards. It occurred to him that all of his recent experiences with Elfish would be good to write about and he wondered if he should actually start another book instead of lying around his house being depressed all the time.

Cary and Lilac arrived. Their heads were always full of dreams but now, having been paid by John Mackie for their first day's work, their current longing for a holiday in the country seemed to be well within their reach. So they carried that dream quite brightly and they also carried with them the sincere best wishes of John Mackie towards Elfish, which they transmitted as she passed them by.

Right at the front of the crowd were Mo and Cody. Their heads being full of marijuana, their dreams were somewhat confused, but Cody had pleasant visions of playing his guitar on stage and being generally admired. Mo shared Cody's rock and roll fantasies but a more pressing concern was to humiliate Elfish.

"Have you met my friend?" he said loudly, grabbing Elfish's arm as she passed. Elfish halted. She glanced at the woman beside Mo who wore sunglasses as black as her own and a floppy hat which concealed all her hair. As Elfish watched she took off her hat and her bright blonde tresses tumbled down over her shoulders.

"Hello, Elfish," said Amnesia. "You don't imitate my voice very well but we both enjoyed your phone calls. Especially when we were fucking."

Amnesia laughed, and so did Mo and Cody. The rest of Mo's band joined in, and then their friends. Elfish suddenly found herself surrounded by a circle of mocking and jeering faces, all of whom had known all along about her attempts at deception.

Elfish was stunned. The laughter grew louder.

"Come on, Elfish," said May, pulling her sleeve, but Elfish was rooted to the spot. She had a disturbingly vivid picture of Mo and Amnesia listening to her phone calls while lying in bed together and the humiliation this caused her was almost too intense to bear.

"Do your Amnesia imitation for me," said Mo, and roared and shook with laughter. Then he leapt up on to the stage, tapped his finger on the singer's microphone to check it was working and announced to the audience that it was now time for Elfish to quote a speech from Shakespeare to them all. The audience, waiting for this moment, went quiet but Mo's entourage kept on laughing. Elfish stood stock still, blinking back a tear behind the sunglasses she had bought with the money she stole from Cary and Lilac.

sixty-five

THE MOMENT ELFISH dragged her body on stage she knew she was going to fail. Standing in front of the microphone she could not prevent herself from trembling. The whole room was now silent, waiting, but the Queen of Dreams could not remember a word.

The silence deepened. Everyone was staring fixedly at Elfish and a new and more sickening humiliation crept up over her.

"Speech!" called Mo, in mockery, bringing renewed laughter from his friends. Elfish scanned her memory with frantic fear, hope and terror but it was useless. She could not recall a single line of Mercutio's speech. The revelation about Amnesia had been too upsetting and the stress thus caused had driven the hard-learned Shakespeare right out of her mind. She stood alone in front of the audience, obviously unable to do what she had publicly promised.

In the hall the silence began to break down into a buzz of conversation punctuated by laughter and some shouts of abuse, all of which made Elfish feel worse. Paralysis took hold of her and she was unable either to speak or move.

"Speech!" cried Mo again. His friends laughed and other people started to join in.

"O! then, I see, Queen Mab hath been with you . . ." shouted

Shonen, prompting her with the first line, but it was hopeless. No power on earth, and not even Queen Mab, could make Elfish remember the speech.

As Elfish stood in silent ignominy, Mo and Cody roared with laughter. Amnesia could barely contain herself and leant on Mo for support, howling with joy.

Elfish remained frozen and terrorised on stage as the laughter spread. Apart from the few supporters she had in the audience, every person in the room now loudly mocked and jeered at her hopelessly inept performance. She found herself in the middle of a nightmare from which she was unable to escape. There seemed to be no way for Elfish to end the situation. She could not even move. Her limbs were paralysed. She would stand there and be ridiculed for the rest of her life.

Eventually, to save his sister from further humiliation, Aran clambered on to the stage and took hold of Elfish's arm. He led her off down the stairs at the side and propelled her through the crowd towards the bar. Elfish allowed herself to be led but she was too distraught to respond to his solicitations. She was acutely aware that her dream had gone. It had flown away to the moon. She could not now call her band Queen Mab. All of her endeavours had been for nothing. At the vital moment she had proved herself to be no better than all the people around her whom she had abused for giving up and accepting defeat.

sixty-six

ELFISH LEANT AGAINST the bar, wreathed in dejection.

"Are you all right?" asked Aran, aware that it was a stupid question.

She shook her head miserably.

"Do you want to leave?"

Elfish did not reply, but placed her hand inside Aran's jacket to remove the small bottle of whisky she knew he was carrying there. Aran, not naturally a generous spirit, let her take it. He could see that all around them people were still looking at Elfish and laughing and he feared that at any moment she might break down entirely. Elfish began pouring the whisky down her throat. Her brother was relieved to see Shonen hurrying towards them. It would surely help if Elfish's friends rallied round.

Unfortunately, Elfish's torments were not yet over. Shonen had not come to rally round.

"I've just been talking to Mo," she exclaimed. "He still says you don't know a fund-raiser. He says you can't help my theatre group. He says you made it all up. Is this true?"

Deep in the misery of defeat and taken by surprise, Elfish found herself unable to lie.

"Yes," she said, without expression.

Shonen turned white and spun on her heel, rushing to vomit in the toilet. Elfish immediately found herself confronted by an angry-looking May and Gail.

"Gail says Chevon isn't moving out of your house and I won't be able to live there!" shouted May at the top of her voice.

"It's true," said Elfish.

"And Mo tells me you've never even met Adam," yelled Gail. "And the talk of benefit gigs for the magazine is a lie."

Elfish's eyes were glazing over. Her reply was too quiet to be heard but it was obvious from her demeanour that she was indeed admitting to lying.

There was no letup. Shonen returned from the toilet to join the others in shouting at her. Elfish quailed. Previously she had been prepared to face down these people when the moment came, confident that once her dream was fulfilled she would have the strength to ignore their fury. Now she could not. Her strength and spirit were both dripping away, leaving her empty inside. She could feel her filth and hunger, and her body was protesting violently about her long period of tension, and drug and alcohol abuse.

Aisha strode up. To anyone familiar with her she had the look of a woman who had managed to control her agoraphobia just long enough to leave the house but knew that it would defeat her before she got back. As she approached, her very limbs were shaking and her face was beginning to distort.

"Where's Mory?" she demanded. "Where is he? He should be here by now."

Elfish felt unable to answer.

"Is he coming? Mo says you didn't even speak to him."

Elfish shook her head, and was forced to endure a fresh torrent of abuse. Aisha, Shonen, Gail and May were all now filled with hate for the woman who had led them on with falsehoods. The room went quiet so that everyone around could hear.

Casaubon, fresh from talking to Mo, marched over to confront Elfish. She saw him coming and felt like an animal trapped in a snare. He pointed a drumstick at her and demanded to know if she had really been in touch with Marcia or was this just another of her lies? When it became obvious that it was, Casaubon's rage was so immediate and violent that Elfish shrank from him and reached backwards to take her brother's hand. Casaubon was very large and Elfish was frightened.

"You fucking little bitch," screamed Casaubon, apparently driven completely mad by the shattered hope of Marcia returning to him. "I could ram this drumstick down your throat! You think you can just lie to people and get them to do what you want and that's all right? I'll kill you for this, Elfish!"

Casaubon, May, Shonen, Aisha and Gail clustered round the small figure of Elfish and screamed at her. The power of the positive transformation that had been wrought on them all was as nothing compared to the fury they displayed as their dreams crashed around their feet before flying with jeers and mockery to lie dormant, wasted and never to be fulfilled, somewhere on the unreachable surface of the moon.

In the face of this assault Elfish crumbled. She turned to face her brother.

"Help me," she said.

Unfortunately, her brother was no longer there. Aran, unable to withstand such violent emotions, had deserted her. He was nowhere to be seen.

At this betrayal by her brother Elfish's spirit collapsed completely and she hung her head and started to cry. While her accusers stood around still screaming at her and the audience listened in with enjoyment, she cried and cried in a public humiliation the like of which had rarely been seen or even imagined by anyone present.

As it seemed that there was now to be no support act playing, the woman behind the mixing desk placed a tape in her machine and Sonic Youth's "Bad Moon Rising" thundered through the speakers.

With their fury still intact but their words for expressing it spent, Shonen, Aisha, Casaubon, May and Gail walked a little distance away then stood together in a knot, still casting evil glances at Elfish. Other onlookers also began to move away from her. They did not wish to find themselves too close to someone so widely condemned and now reduced to the universally dreaded phenomenon of crying in public.

Over in a corner Mo and his band laughed and laughed, and made raucous comments about what Mo might demand from Elfish, should she ever stop crying for long enough to grant it.

sixty-seven

ELFISH WAS LOST. She struggled to halt her tears. There was now nothing for her to do except finish Aran's whisky and go home. When Mo appeared in front of her and congratulated her on her performance she was incapable of even making a reply. When he told her how happy he was to call his band Queen Mab she remained mute. Even the sight of Amnesia, gloating, could not make her react.

Someone touched her shoulder from behind and spoke in her ear.

"What time are you playing, Elfish?"

Who could be stupid enough to ask such a question? Turning round, Elfish was not surprised to find that it was Cary and Lilac.

She blinked, trying to clear the tears and grime from her eyes, and wiped a long trail of mucus away from her nose with her sleeve.

"What time are you going on, Elfish? We want to hear you play."

Elfish shook her head and told them she was not playing. She no longer had a band to play with, she no longer had the desire to play and even if she did no one would want to hear her.

"But you have to play," said Cary. "That's why we came."

"And John Mackie said to be sure and encourage you. Thanks for getting us the job with him."

Having just suffered the worst experience of her life, Elfish was in no mood to indulge such foolishness. She was irritated beyond belief by their ridiculous good humour and snapped at them, telling them to go away and leave her alone. This had no effect.

"We want to hear you," they said.

"That's why we came."

"Will you leave me alone?" demanded Elfish. "I can't stand the way you keep being friendly to me all the time. Haven't you noticed how much I detest you?"

It was no use. Cary and Lilac possessed an unbreakable force-field of benevolent optimism. They laughed off Elfish's aggression, assuming she did not really mean it.

"So are you going to play soon?"

"Aaahhh!" screamed Elfish, tormented again, and felt a desperate desire to stop these people from liking her.

"My sunglasses," she gasped, in desperation. "You know how I paid for them?"

"How?"

"I stole your money. I dug it up from your garden and stole it."

Cary and Lilac's eyes widened.

"You didn't."

"I did."

"You couldn't."

Elfish stared at them.

A tear trickled down Lilac's cheek. This treacherous action was too much even for him. Cary sniffed. It was almost impossible for her to believe that Elfish could have done such a thing. Despite all of Elfish's abuse, she had actually thought they were friends.

Wordless and in tears they turned and left.

Well, right, thought Elfish, and felt slightly better. I finally managed to annoy Cary and Lilac.

Belly's "Low Red Moon" sounded loud in the room and smoke hung thick around the tables. Small fingers clutched at Elfish's jacket.

"It's all right, Elfish," said Cary. "We don't mind."

"I suppose you needed the money," said Lilac. "And after all, you got us the job."

"I didn't get you the job!"

"Well, we got it because we were friends of yours."

They smiled at her.

"So when are you going to play?"

Elfish was truly astonished. She stared at their eager young faces and grubby white dreadlocks and marvelled at them. And in a moment of revelation she saw quite clearly that Cary and Lilac had a dream that everything was fine and everyone liked them and no matter how ludicrous this dream was they were not going to be dissuaded from it. They had apparently made up their minds to believe it and that was that.

She was abruptly ashamed that she had been dissuaded from her own dream. After all, what did she, Elfish, care what people thought? Not caring what people thought was one of Elfish's strongest points. Looking around the bar she saw her detractors in every corner and she was furious. She was furious with them and furious with herself. Her mind cleared quite suddenly and her spirit revived. She straightened up, took a deep breath, finished Aran's whisky, dropped the bottle so it smashed on the floor and spat in the direction of Mo.

"I think I'll go and play right now."

Using her boots and elbows Elfish burrowed her way violently to the stage. She leapt on to it with the power and grace of a seasoned stage diver. She picked up her guitar, turned up the volume till it shrieked with feedback then shouted through the microphone for the sound woman to turn it up further.

Dissatisfied with her fuzzbox she stamped on it and kicked it viciously till it spluttered into overdrive, thus gaining the attention of the crowd. She then began to declaim her speech, punctuating each line with a horribly distorted chord so that the audience shifted around in fear and discomfort. She placed her fingers randomly on the fretboard, creating dreadful clashing disharmonies and each one of these she pulled further into chaos with the tremolo arm on her guitar. These dreadful chords shrieked and whirled around the room, feeding back on each other till the noise was truly dreadful, a fantastical and grotesque cacophony that could never have been imagined and could never be repeated. Elfish roared her Queen Mab speech over the top of this brutal sonic attack, delivering Shakespeare in a uniquely effective and violent manner.

The audience, protesting at first, were soon beaten into submission. They huddled close to their loved ones for protection and gazed in wonder. As the speech came to an end Elfish mouthed a few lines of foul abuse at them all and plunged into her favourite song, "Here Comes the Moon." Halfway through it she abandoned singing and, still playing her guitar with one hand, began to climb the speaker stack at the side of the stage. It lurched and swayed as she made the ascent and the audience began to cheer.

"Queen Mab, the deliverer of dreams," cried Elfish. High above the concrete floor, guitar in hand, she leapt out into space in a stage dive that was both utterly spectacular and completely suicidal.

sixty-eight

ELFISH HUNG IN the air. She was weighed down and seriously encumbered by her guitar. The strap and lead, already tangling round her neck and legs, would prevent her from adopting any sort of sensible landing position. A disastrous headfirst collision with the grey concrete floor was only seconds away.

While she hung in the air a variety of thoughts raced through the minds of those present, ranging from a mild desire on the part of Mo that Elfish should not actually kill herself to a terrible fear on the part of Aran that she might.

Aran was well aware that he had deserted Elfish when she needed him. Although he would later claim that he had merely visited the cigarette machine after suffering an overpowering urge to have one last try for card number twenty, he knew that really his nerve had failed him. As Elfish flew to her doom he felt bitter regret. He loved his sister and he had to acknowledge that without her he would still be sitting depressed in his gloomy living room. Heedless of his own safety he rushed forward to catch her.

Elfish's ex-collaborators, still standing in an angry circle, had similar feelings.

Oh dear, thought Shonen, as Elfish hung at the apex of her leap.

Elfish has lied to me and deceived me. But where would I be if she had not? Stuck in a cycle of vomiting and hating myself. Now I have filled in all my sponsorship applications and my theatre group is back together. This would never have happened without Elfish. Shonen rushed forward to catch her.

Oh, no, thought Aisha, as Elfish began her descent. Elfish is going to kill herself. And Elfish has misled me cruelly about Mory coming back but there again where would I be if she had not? I was sitting in my flat, too scared to even visit the shops or even get out of bed, and now I have painted a backdrop and come to the gig and enjoyed myself and things do not seem too bad, really. Not wishing that Elfish should kill herself, Aisha rushed forward to catch her.

Hell! thought May. That idiot Elfish is going to break her stupid neck and despite the fact that she deceived me about getting me a place to live I enjoy playing guitar with her. I have never had so much fun as during this last week of rehearsing. So May also rushed forward to catch her.

Gail, a person who had suffered a great deal at Elfish's hands, was nonetheless consumed with guilt at the sight of Elfish plummeting towards disaster. After all, it was undoubtedly true that Gail and her friends would have given up entirely on the magazine had it not been for Elfish. Lies or not, it had spurred them on to action. Now they were all doing layouts and writing articles and the whole thing was almost ready to roll off the presses. Gail rushed forward to rescue Elfish.

Casaubon, cruelly disappointed in love, still hated Elfish but he did not wish to be left behind. Additionally, he had an image of himself as a large, strong, male drummer. He felt that he really should not let a small woman fall to her death in front of his eyes. When Elfish was nearing the floor, he hurled himself into action.

Seeing all this the figure of Queen Mab, resplendent on the backdrop, smiled to herself, and was satisfied. Or so Elfish thought later anyway, from the brief glimpse she had of her as she hurtled head over heels towards the ground.

The rescuers were determined in spirit but uncoordinated in action. During the headlong rush May tripped over Aran who sprawled under Aisha. Gail, Shonen and Casaubon crashed into them and all six lay in a painful struggling heap in front of the stage.

Elfish, by luck, although she later claimed it as deliberate, had now somersaulted entirely and, like a diver who has successfully completed a complicated series of twists and turns in the air before ending up in precisely the right position to enter the water, landed safely. She came to ground on her feet, knees slightly bent, rather like an experienced parachute jumper. She was jarred by the impact, but unharmed.

Elfish gazed at the struggling mass of bodies in front of her.

"Well, thank you," she said. "You saved my life."

"You stupid bitch, Elfish," said May, disentangling herself from the melee. She glowered at Aran, swore loudly, then proceeded to haul herself on stage where she unceremoniously plugged in her guitar and started to play. Gail followed her. After a brief hesitation Casaubon did likewise and the band lurched into their first number, a numbingly loud cover version of Ministry's "Jesus Built My Hot Rod." Elfish, after some confusion while she unwrapped her guitar lead from round her neck, made it back on stage, planted herself in front of the microphone and began to sing.

By now the audience was in a frenzy, having witnessed the most spectacular introduction to a gig ever seen in Brixton. Already mesmerised by Elfish's jarring performance of Shakespeare they were thrilled beyond measure by her spectacular stage dive and the scramble that followed. Consequently they were more than willing to give a sympathetic listening to the band, although, being under-rehearsed, they were still not very good.

sixty-nine

SO ELFISH GOT to call her band Queen Mab, as Cary and Lilac happily reported to John Mackie later. They themselves had not rushed forward to save her because they had assumed that, as an experienced stage diver, Elfish knew what she was doing. They continued to hide their savings in the tin in the garden, confidently assuming that the money would now be safe. Unwise, perhaps, with Elfish living next door, but they were like that.

Although Elfish seemed to be forgiven by those people she had lied to, she was not forgiven by Tula and Lizzy for her behaviour towards May. It is often the way that the friends of the victim will go on being resentful long after the victim herself has forgotten all about it. Elfish would not admit to caring either way.

She was gloriously happy after her success, so happy that on her next visit to Aran she allowed him to put her in the bath, from where she emerged clean but melancholy.

"Now I've achieved what I wanted to achieve I don't know what to do," she said.

Aran refrained from any useless advice, knowing that Elfish would simply carry on as usual for a while, drinking and playing pool, before finding the urge to get on with things again, particularly as she now had a band to look after. This would no doubt involve much trauma, and probably the violent abuse and sacking of all the members, and would suit Elfish fine. So he diverted her attention from her melancholy with a cheerful tale about the arrest, trial and execution of some Athenian captains, and asked her if she would be willing to encourage her band to smoke a little more. He was still on the trail of card number twenty, and time was running out.

As for Mo, he was surprised to find that he did not mind too much how things had turned out. He had to find another name for his band but the world was full of names. Every day Cody would suggest a new one, usually with some reference to Ben Jonson or some other unsuitable person. Mo rejected all of these, but something would turn up. Furthermore, he was very happy with Amnesia. They made an excellent couple, and while no one was about to give Elfish any credit for this, it could well be said that she was responsible for bringing them together.